Michas

SECRETS AND SPIES

A Scottish Wartime Mystery

Mary S. Rosambeau (signature)

By

Mary Rosambeau

ISBN: 978-1-5272-3373-7

First published 2019

Secrets and Spies is a work of historical fiction. Although the events described loosely follow real-life scenarios, the characters within this book are not representative of any person, alive or dead, and are purely fictional constructs.

Acknowledgements

One day, Kezmon, a member of my local primary school reading group, asked me to find him a Second World War story that was not about the London Blitz. He was curious to know what wartime was like in other parts of Britain during the war. This question was the inspiration for *Secrets and Spies*.

I have had so much help and encouragement with my writing that it is difficult to be sure no one has been left out.

I should perhaps first thank my brother Kenneth, whose schoolboy wartime adventures in our small Scottish village, gave me the idea on which the story is based.

My writers group helped hone the first drafts. Special thanks go to Sally Rowe, Sally Purdie, Kate Charmain, and Toni Allen, who all helped open my eyes to the art of writing.

No children's book should go out into the world without having been read first by at least one child. Oliver Banham was my first draft reader. His comment, that he'd recommend it to the boys in his class, encouraged me to carry on.

Callum, Seth, Danny, and all the members of my reading group at Potley Hill Primary school proved to be wonderful editors. They thought a glossary and some historical notes should be added, and it was at their suggestion that I drew the illustrations.

Finally, I must thank Jordan, my adult editor and mentor for keeping me on track, my husband Peter for doing the cooking while I sat glued to the computer, and you, my readers, without whom no book would exist.

Chapter 1

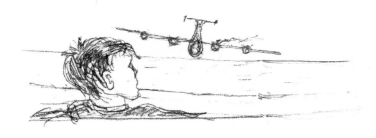

Rory ducked behind the sea wall and stared upwards. Surely that Lancaster Bomber was flying in far too low? The thunderous noise of the plane's engines was deafening. As it passed, it left a thick, black metallic trail across the bright summer sky. The plane was in trouble. Coughing as the smoky tang caught in his throat, Rory turned to follow its progress across the bay towards the Air Force base. He dug his fingers into the gritty stone of the ancient wall, watching the plane stutter and stumble through the sky.

'Come on... Come on...' he muttered, urging it onwards.

The plane dropped in the sky, recovered again, swayed, tilted, and finally managed to make an awkward turn inland. It disappeared. Rory held his breath. Seconds passed, then minutes, but no explosion. No fire. It must have landed safely.

Folding like a burst balloon, Rory breathed again. He collapsed heavily against the wall, enjoying the cool spray kicked up by the waves. As his heart rate slowed, he started to laugh, wishing someone else had seen this, and could share the excitement with him.

But maybe someone had.

Leaping up, he took off. He stretched out his arms and ran down the pavement. He was a legendary pilot, zooming through the air, swerving to shoot down an imaginary swarm of enemies. Over his shoulder, German fighter planes disappeared in a puff of black smoke and ack-ack gunfire.

'Keep up, Spitfire Squadron,' he called. 'Cover my tail!'

Along the front, past a neat row of fishermen's cottages, he ran. Without stopping, he vaulted the garden gate, and thundered up the stairs to Dad's study.

'Dad!' he shouted on his way up, 'Dad! Dad! Did you see that plane?'

Just as he reached the top step, the study door slammed shut. From inside came Dad's voice, 'Not now Rory!'

No one argued with that tone.

Stranded on the landing, Rory's pretend plane crashed. His shoulders slumped. Balling his fists, he pulled the most hideous, awful face he could manage. Even if Dad had someone in there with him, why not just say so? No need to shout; no need to make him feel like a silly little boy being a nuisance.

'I hate this place!' Rory mouthed at the closed door. Everything had gone wrong since they'd moved north from Edinburgh. Why did they have to end up in this nothing-wee-village? It was all very well for his parents – always busy with their jobs. But why should he, Rory, have been uprooted from school and forced to leave all his old friends? It wasn't fair.

He turned back downstairs, and deliberately slid from one step to the next, in the way that Mum always said would wear out the carpet. *Too bad,* he thought, *she's not here…too busy at that smelly baby clinic.*

Rory jumped the last step, slammed the front door behind him, and stopped in surprise. Paul, his one new friend, was coming in through the gate. He had a bait box tucked in the fingers of his paralysed hand.

'Fancy a bit of fishing?'

Rory grinned. At last, someone who wanted to spend time with him.

'Just get my gear,' he said, reaching through the open

shed door for his fishing tackle bucket. 'Did you see that plane a minute ago? I thought it was going to crash.'

'Yeah! Brilliant, wasn't it? It must have been okay though, or we'd have heard the fire siren even from here. D'you think it got hit?'

'Dunno, maybe just engine trouble. Jerries don't usually fly this far north. Be great if he'd escaped an attack...' Rory swung his bucket, '...let's be fighters chasing Jerry off. You be a Spitfire? I'm a Hurricane. Race you to the pier!'

Rory was winning. Already he could see the end of the sea wall. But what was that? He stopped so suddenly that Paul cannoned right into him, knocking the wind out of both of them.

'Hey!' Paul could barely stay upright. 'What's up?'

'Look at that,' Rory glared, pointing. There'd been nothing here earlier. Now someone had put up a big sign, in fresh red paint – *No Fishing!*

Rory kicked the sea wall. 'It's this war!' he said, slouching to the ground. 'Here's another thing we're not allowed to do!'

'Yeah,' Paul was giving the notice a black look, 'but how could our fishing hurt anybody?'

'I don't think it's about fishing at all. I bet it's to keep us away, because there's something hush-hush going on.'

'Like what?'

'Well, could be something to do with that strange trawler that's started to come in?' Rory reached for his bucket. 'Anyway, never mind them,' he said. 'We're still going to fish, but down below, out of sight.' He hitched the bucket up onto his arm, 'That way we can fish *and* see anything that's going on - especially if that boat comes in again.'

Savouring the chance of forbidden adventure, Paul took a quick glance around. No sign of Groucho Main, the harbour master. The docks were almost completely empty, save for a few seagulls, wheeling like kites over the water.

'All clear,' said Paul.

Rory, now a special agent on a mission, swung himself under the wooden walkway. He perched on one of the thick timbers that pinned the walkway to the sea wall. Down here, in this great, dark, echoey place, their fishing lines would drop into the water with barely a splash. Better still, if they sat well back, with their legs dangling over the dangerous swell of deep water, they wouldn't be seen.

Agile as a monkey, despite his bad arm, Paul was down beside him. 'Budge up,' he said.

Taking a breath of the dank air, Rory shuffled along. He smiled. He remembered the day Paul had plumped into the empty school desk beside him. Ignoring the giggling whispers about "Captain Hook-hand" being placed next to "Holy Joe", they'd hit it off immediately. Together, they'd managed to fend off the taunts of school bullies – "spastic", "new boys". A few well-aimed kicks from Rory, and a flurry of punches from Paul's good hand, was more than enough. Nowadays, their classmates left them well alone. Besides, Rory thought, the sons of a minister and the new village policeman could have just as much fun ignoring a *Keep Out* sign as anyone else.

'Now,' he said, threading a wriggling lugworm onto his friend's hook, a fiddly job for Paul's twisted fingers. 'What do you know about this strange boat...called *The Christian* or something?'

'You mean *The Kirsten,*' said Paul, tying the hook and heavy sinker to his line, with his good hand. He fiddled for a moment, then dropped the line into the green depths below. 'They're not strange, stupid, they're Norwegian. Norway's on our side in the war, so why would their being here be hush-hush?'

'I know that, silly,' groaned Rory. 'My mum's Norwegian and they're the best. What I mean is, why would they use a wee harbour like ours rather than a big port like Wick or Aberdeen?' All of a sudden, Rory flexed his line. He had a bite already!

'That's just a tiddler!' Paul scoffed. He helped Rory

pull the line out of the water. It was indeed a tiddler.

Rory popped the little flat fish into his bucket. 'Don't you worry my wee fishy,' he told it, 'you'll soon have company in there.'

He looked up. A seagull was edging its way towards the bucket. Rory shooed it away. They watched as it took off, skimming over the glass-green surface of the water. It wheeled down to join a squawking chorus of its friends, gossiping along the harbour wall.

Paul got two bites, one after the other, while Rory cast again.

'I bet there is something secret going on with that *Kirsten*,' Rory continued, dropping another fish into the bucket, 'but there's been no whisper round the playground. You know our lot are always on about the latest hush-hush stuff.'

'Yeah, but they're only interested in the new Canadian soldiers with their jeeps and trucks. They hang around them all day, asking stupid questions. Any gum, chum? Give us a lift in your lorry? No chance.'

'I guess the Norwegians must hate the Germans,' Rory said, reaching for the bait tin. 'Imagine how we'd feel if the tanks rolled in here!' He shivered at the idea.

'Why would the Nazis bother with us up here in Scotland?' said Paul. 'Don't worry, it's only London and big towns they're bombing.'

'Suppose so,' said Rory, shrugging it off, 'but I bet that boat's coming here for a reason.'

'Okay, let's just watch for it. No one can see us up here.'

'Just as well, if anyone saw where we are, and told on us, our mums would have a fit.'

'But Darlings, so dangerous!' Paul screeched. They both fell about laughing, to the extent that Rory nearly fell off the bar.

'You're right, you know,' said Rory, recovering his breath, and his balance. 'This is a great place to see all around. Look at that brilliant view over the bay to the sand dunes.' He pointed off in the distance. Even from this far out, they could see the big red signs barring entrance to the beach – *DANGER! KEEP OUT! LIVE ROUNDS!* Rory checked his line again, 'Pity only the army can go there now. Before the war they say it was an ace place for adventures.'

Paul thought for a moment, 'Wouldn't it be some adventure, just to creep in under their great barbed wire fencing, in spite of all the notices?'

'How mad are you, Paul? Live rounds means you really could be killed by a landmine!'

Paul did come up with some daft ideas. But it was

unfair; blocking off their beach had left only the Hart Hill woods as a place to play. Even so, Rory was proud of the secret camouflaged-camp he and Paul had built there. They had a new commando game, creeping silently through the heather, from tree to tree – an imaginary army of two.

Paul stood up. Steadying himself against the wall, he hauled his line in. 'Got to go, chum. Mum said five o'clock and no later – you staying on for a bit?'

'Yeah, my mum's helping in the forces' canteen, and my dad's got a church prayer meeting. No one's gonna miss me.'

'Right then,' said Paul, fixing the hook into his ball of line. 'Come round early tomorrow so we can finish the go-kart. All we need now is rope to steer her. I asked Mum for a bit of washing line but no luck.'

'You were lucky to find the old pram wheels at the dump,' said Rory.

'Yeah, otherwise Charlie Munro and his gang would have had them.'

Rory looped a bit of twine through the gills of Paul's catch so he could carry them. Paul hung the bundle from his bad hand.

'See you tomorrow, chum!' One handed, Paul hoisted himself up onto the pier with a wiggle and a kick.

Rory checked what was left in the bucket. Even his dad

would have to agree he'd done well. Cleaned and gutted, these three would make a good fry up. He tipped the tiddler back into the sea with a splash, tied the rest together, and prepared to pull himself up onto the pier. Then, all of a sudden, he froze.

Quite near, and getting nearer, came the distinctive tonk-tonk engine noise of a Norwegian trawler. As the boat came closer, Rory could read the name printed neatly along her side. It was *The Kirsten.* She was coming in quite quickly. The high wash of her bow wave was even now splashing against the pier. Mobbed by a cloud of screaming seagulls, she was already at the harbour mouth. In she came, chugging by, close to where he stood on the bar.

Chapter 2

As the boat came past, a young, fair-haired seaman waved from the deck. Gripping the timber to keep his balance, Rory waved back with the hand that held his fish. The man laughed and sent a thumbs-up in praise of his catch, as the boat swept on.

Rory's smile turned to an expression of horror. He should have hidden, not waved. He wasn't meant to be there. And suddenly, it got worse. Old Grouch Main, the Harbour Master, was standing at his office window – glaring straight at Rory. He'd been seen!

Snatching his gear, Rory scrambled onto the pier and pelted along the quay. Mr Main was already out of his office, shouting, 'Stop right there, you little varmit!'

The Kirsten's mooring ropes were being thrown. Not paying attention where he was going, Rory tripped on them. Trying to save himself, he dropped his catch in the water.

'Ow, ow-ow!' he gashed his knee as he fell.

'Serves you right, you little beggar!' roared Old Grouch, who'd been just about to grab him. Instead, someone else had hold of him. Another hand helped him to his feet. It belonged to the fisherman who'd waved from the boat. Rory ducked behind him.

'Come on, Captain,' the Norwegian was saying, 'let him free this time'. His soft accent made the request sound reasonable. 'He's had punish enough to lose his fish, and see, he's bleeding.'

Rory looked down. It was true. Yuk! He shivered. A thick trickle of blood poured down his leg into his sock. Mr Main hesitated, grunted, then waved a stubby finger.

'Lucky for you, Rory McKay, this gentleman has spoken for you. Just don't let me catch you fishing from

there again, or I'll be telling your dad.'

With another grunt and a snort he turned away to deal with the newly berthed Norwegian trawler. Rory came out from behind his rescuer.

'Thanks,' he said. 'You saved my life. If Mr Main had told my dad he'd have gone mad. He's always on about my behaviour reflecting badly on him and the church.'

The seaman grinned.

'I just thought, how hard, you lose that very good catch of fish,' he said. 'If you wait here, I find you more...yes?'

The man jumped back into the boat and picked up a rucksack. He put his hand into a box – coming out with three herrings, which he put into a sheet of newspaper. When he came back, Rory was wiping his leg with a hanky.

The man dropped his rucksack and parcel.

'Here,' he said, 'I can do that.'

He dabbed Rory's knee dry, then twisted the handkerchief into a makeshift bandage. Straightening up, he retrieved his bag and handed Rory the parcel of fish.

'Here, have these to replace these ones you lost,' he said.

'But that's part of your catch, shouldn't I pay?' said Rory.

'No lad, these were only for show.'

He bent a bit closer and Rory caught the peaty smoke

smell from his knitted jumper. The man turned and pointed over his shoulder at the boat. His blue eyes crinkled at the corners as he whispered, 'Look, this crew weren't after fish, they were fishing for men.'

"Fishing for men?' Rory frowned.

Following the man's finger, he saw a line of people coming up from the boat. They were weary-looking – men, women and children – all straggled out on the quay, huddled together.

'They were almost all seasick on the way over,' the man said, 'but they'll be all right now. See, someone has come to meet them. I was fished up too, you know. I will join them later. But I have something to fetch first. Can you help? I need to find the forces' canteen.'

'Yes, of course,' said Rory, happy to have something he could do to repay the man for his help. 'It's on my way home. What do you mean they were fished up?'

'We're refugees, from Norway, escaping the Nazis. Now we've been saved.'

Rory frowned again. Refugees? But, surely saving them was a good thing. Why should it be hush-hush?

'I'm half Norwegian myself. My mum's from Norway, and even though she's lived here for years, it still makes her sad it's fallen to the Nazis. Were they after you?'

'Oh, yes.' The man gave that crinkly smile again. 'The

Nazis think I am a very bad boy.'

'What did you do?' Rory didn't know if one should ask personal questions, but how could he resist?

'Careless talk costs lives,' said the man. For a moment, Rory thought that this was just like something his dad would say, but then he realised that the man was smiling down at him, tapping a finger to the side of his nose. Wow! At last, here was an adult treating him as a friend.

The man waved goodbye to a crewman on the boat, then turned to Rory, 'Shall we go?' Rory squared his shoulders with pride. They were a team.

'This way,' Rory said, setting off to show the way up Harbour Lane, onto the high street. They turned right at the red telephone box, with its big poster warning those who used it to take care – just in case spies were listening in.

'The doctor has the only other telephone,' said Rory, 'except of course, the one in the police station.'

They could now look straight down the road to the end of the village.

'It's not difficult to find your way,' said Rory, pointing. 'That's the coast guard station behind us on the headland.'

The Norwegian man glanced back.

'Oh yes,' he said, 'I saw it from the boat as we came in, built right on the edge of your brilliant cliffs. Do people around here go climbing? I'd love to have a go at them. We could try climbing together one day, if you fancy.'

Excitement zipped through Rory's veins. This man was more like an older brother than an adult.

'I'd love that,' he said, bouncing off the pavement into the road as they walked along. 'I've never gone rock climbing before.'

Turning to avoid a group of people chatting outside the post office, Rory remembered that he was meant to be helping the man find his way around the village. 'That's the post office,' he said, 'and there's the Village Hall, at the foot of the hill. That's where they hold your forces' canteen. It's right opposite the church with the square tower. Next door to that is the Manse, where I live, and just on a bit is the police station.'

'Big tower on your church,' said the Norwegian. 'Can

you climb that?'

'Oh yes,' said Rory, 'but it's not like rock climbing. It's got a narrow stairway. There's just one bell left now. It's only to be rung if the Germans invade.'

He hopped on and off the pavement as they walked along, and since the man seemed interested in the bell tower, he continued:

'Before the war we had a peal of four bells, but then the army came and took them for scrap. They made a great mess taking them down. One of them fell and crashed through the loft floor. It made the most humungous hole!'

'Three whole bells! I expect other stuff went for scrap as well?'

'Oh, yes. Not long after I started school, one playtime, they came with acetylene torches to cut down the school railings. It made great showers of sparks and they fell like great chopped off chunks of hair! Then they piled them all up on a lorry with the bells and drove off.' He grinned at the memory of that exciting day.

'Where were they taken?'

Rory looked up, puzzled. Why would anyone want to know that?

'Somewhere they could be melted down and made into tanks, I expect,' he said with a shrug.

'And do they make tanks near here?'

'No!' Rory laughed at the idea. 'This is the middle of nowhere. I don't think there's a factory for a hundred miles. We've only got forests and farms round here.'

They stopped at the village hall.

'The forces' canteen is held in here,' he said. 'My mum's helping out tonight. I'd introduce you, but I don't know your name.'

'You can call me Sven.'

The hall door was opening. Rory saw his mum about to come out. Surprised to see him, she gave an angry glance at her watch.

'Is this you just coming home now?' she said. 'It's nearly six o'clock.'

'Sorry, Mum, I fell over at the harbour. This nice man helped me up and gave me these herring when I lost my fish.'

She bent down to check Rory's grubby bandage.

'That'll need a wash, but a plaster will probably fix it. Thank you for your help, Mr...'

But while they'd been busy with Rory's knee, Sven had disappeared into the hall.

'Oh, never mind,' said Mum, as Rory looked around to see where Sven had gone, 'you can find him tomorrow to thank him, but Rory, I've got to get supper ready, so right now we need to go home.'

Rory thought she looked tired. Despite being cross with her earlier, he knew minister's wives were expected to do everything. His mum helped with church meetings as well as her war work. He vowed to give her a hand by setting the table tonight.

As soon as they opened the front door they were met by the delicious smell of Mum's rabbit stew.

'Yummee!' Rory shouted, kicking off his shoes and sliding along the shiny lino in his socks.

'Slippers, Rory,' his mum called after him, still hanging up her coat.

Rory found his slippers by the kitchen fireplace. Having wriggled into them, he laid the packet of fish by the side of the sink. He flipped the table cloth from the drawer, and by the time his mum reached the kitchen, he'd nearly finished laying the table.

'Well done, Rory,' she said, bending to take the casserole from the oven.

As she straightened up, Rory noticed she'd seen the packet of fish by the sink. He hurried to explain.

'That's the fish the man gave me when I fell and dropped mine in the water.'

'I'm not sure I want you getting too friendly with fishermen.'

'But…he was nice. He didn't have to give me the fish.

Look, Mum, they're proper herring, far better than the flounders I'd caught.'

He unfolded the newspaper and for a change, Mum looked impressed.

'I'll clean them for you,' he offered. Noting that this won him a smile, he took another shot.

'Mum, is it alright if I go round to Paul's tomorrow? We're going to finish his go-kart, and he was asking if we might have any rope. Do you think we could have one of the old bell ropes from the loft?'

Mum was putting on her apron.

'The old bell ropes? Yes, I think that would be alright, but remind me in the morning. You're not to go up by yourself. It's quite dangerous. We'll go up together.'

At the sound of the front door they both paused.

'Dad's home,' said Rory, bouncing up, keen to tell Dad about his afternoon adventure. His father, still in his black Sunday suit and white dog collar, hurried into the kitchen. Without noticing Rory, he went straight over to Mum.

'Any news of our friend yet?' he asked. Mum shook her head. Dad frowned, 'There must be some difficulty with his cover. I hope they know the boat won't wait forever.'

Dad looked anxious, so Rory guessed this wasn't the time to bother him with tales of fishing...but someone who needed cover sounded interesting. He was just about to ask what it meant when Dad turned around. He looked startled to see Rory there.

'Rory! Sorry, I didn't notice you. Homework all done?'

'Oh, Dad, we're on holiday – the potato holidays, you know? October, *tattie howking week.'*

Dad looked blank. 'Oh yes, of course,' he said, remembering. 'I can't get used to the idea of children being sent to pick potatoes. At least you're only eleven, not old enough for that yet, so I hope you made profitable use of your free time.'

And then he was gone up to his study. The door clicked shut before Rory had a chance to tell him that he'd 'profitably' spent his time, to the tune of three whole herring.

'Never mind,' said Mum, who must have noticed his disappointment. 'We'll tell him about them tomorrow when I serve them for supper. Now, let's have a look at that knee.'

He sat down for her to clean it up.

'You're a good boy, Rory,' she said, applying a plaster. 'Don't mind Dad being so short with you, he has a lot on his mind right now. You needn't worry about the fish. I'll clean them tonight.

Dad brought papers with him to the table. Sometimes he would even continue to study his papers while he ate, making notes with a thick black pencil, but tonight he laid them aside.

'I met your friend Paul when I called on PC Gordon just now,' Dad remarked. 'He'd made a good catch of fish. His dad's very proud that he can manage his fishing tackle unaided, despite his paralysed hand.'

'Polio was it?' asked Mum.

'Apparently Paul was so ill they nearly lost him, but now his disability doesn't stop him doing anything. I'm glad he's your friend, Rory. You could learn a thing or two from him.'

Rory stared. If Dad only knew some of the utterly daft things he had to *stop* Paul from doing.

'Well,' said Mum, intervening, 'Paul's probably got to show everyone he's as good as other boys who might bully him. Rory did catch fish too, you know.'

Rory smiled at his mum.

'Yes, but he's more capable, so that's not quite the same,' said Dad, picking up his papers and changing the subject. 'The settlement officer said more Norwegian refugees arrived this evening. He was looking for people to take them in like the evacuees from Glasgow.'

'The WRVS has been collecting clothes...'

'Mum?' Rory interrupted his parents. 'Norwegians who come here are on our side, aren't they?'

'What's this about, Rory? Have you met some Norwegians?'

Mum was so busy serving out rhubarb crumble that she didn't seem to notice his failure to reply. From now on, he resolved, he'd keep quiet about Sven. Mum said she didn't want him befriending fishermen, but she'd also said he should thank Sven tomorrow. And he intended to do just that.

Chapter 3

The next morning was Mum's wash day, so before Rory could give any thought to ropes or go-karts, there were chores to be done. While Mum stripped the bed, Rory bundled up the sheets, so he could take them down to the boiler in the wash house at the back of the Manse. Rory enjoyed wrestling the great tangles of linen over the side of the metal cauldron. Then, like a fireman called to save a burning house, he ran to fill the buckets of water to splosh over them, so they could soak.

Fireman's work finished, he became Rory the magician, with a big cup of sharp smelling soap flakes to stir into

the brew. Now for the best bit: the fire drawer had to be pulled out from under the boiler. Tipping the old ashes into a bucket, he banged the box to make sure it was clean. Now he was a resistance fighter, crouched behind Nazi headquarters, about to set a fire to push under their floor. He laid a bed of crushed newspaper, then sticks, and on top put nuggets of coal to catch once the sticks were alight. All was ready. His first match blew out. He could hear footsteps. Quick, quick, or he'd be caught.

He touched the next match to the paper. The bright yellow flame ate into the sticks. A gentle push and in went the fire down the tunnel. The drawer clicked into place under the copper boiler, flames flared up, and the water began to heat.

Hush! More Nazi footsteps...no, all safe, it was only Mum.

'Well done, Rory,' she said. Her hair was tied neatly in a headscarf, as though ready to go out. 'We'll check to make sure it's still going once we've been up the tower.'

Mum had remembered the rope! She had the key in her hand.

The Manse where they lived was next to the church. They had only to cross the garden. Rory always loved the approach to the tower door. It made him think of words from that old Scottish ballad: *"Childe Rowland to the dark*

tower came..."

This could be the dark tower, and as Childe Rowland, what adventure might await him there?

Mum frowned as the key rattled in the lock.

'Rory, this door isn't locked, how odd. I didn't think anyone used it these days.'

Pocketing the key, she went in and began to climb up the spiral staircase ahead of him. It was so narrow that all he could see were her shoes disappearing as he followed round each turn. She said something above him. He didn't hear properly and was about to say, 'What?' when, BUMP, THUMP...

'Rory!' Mum screamed, falling backwards towards him.

He leapt aside, but not fast enough. Her head caught the wall with a vicious THWAK. She rolled over onto her side, with her legs splayed out beneath her.

'Mum!' he yelled. 'Mum, are you alright?'

Her eyes were open, but they looked dazed and vacant. She didn't move. Blood, from a deep cut on her head, ran down the side of her face, creating a pool on the step below.

Suddenly, someone was pushing at him from behind, trying to get past, to reach her.

'Go!' said a familiar voice, 'Run for help!'

Rory turned and looked into the face of Sven. Except now he wasn't cool, calm and collected like the previous night. He was frantic, bending down over Rory's mother, trying to stop the blood pouring from her head. There was no time for Rory to wonder what he was doing there.

'No,' cried Rory in anguish, holding fast to his mum's hands, 'I can't leave her!' Then, as Sven seemed to hesitate, he shouted at him in desperation, 'I *have* to stay with her. You go!'

Sven ran.

'Mum. Oh, Mum, wake up!'

Rory tried to control his breathing but it was coming in gasps. Was she dead? He leaned his cheek against hers and then, thank goodness, he felt a soft breath.

'Hurry, hurry! Someone help!'

'Rory?'

A voice from the garden called up the stairs. Paul's voice! He'd probably got tired of waiting for him at the house.

'Quick, Paul, can you get help? Mum's fallen down the stairs and hit her head.'

'I'll get my dad. There might be a Red Cross doctor in the forces' cafe. Hang on in there. I'll be back.'

Rory listened to the sound of Paul's running feet, first along the gravel drive, then out the gate and pattering on the pavement. Soon, soon, he'd bring someone back.

Rory looked around. What ought he to be doing while waiting for someone to come? He tried to ease his mum's legs into a more comfortable position. If only he hadn't flattened himself against the wall when she fell, he thought, trembling with guilt, he could have stopped her hitting her head.

'Oh, Mum, what have I done?' he groaned, cradling her.

'Rory, what's going on?' His father's angry shout echoed up the stairwell. He must have been on his way into the church and seen the tower door open. 'How many times have I told you not to climb up there?'

'Dad, Dad, it's Mum. She's hurt. She fell on the steps. Paul's gone for help.'

Dad's head and shoulders were suddenly crushed into the space beside him.

'Greta!' he gasped, his voice cracking, 'Come, lad, help me get her down from here.'

Reaching past him, his father grasped the shoulders of Mum's jacket, propped her gently against him and began to move backwards. Rory caught her feet to stop them clunking on the steps. In slow, awkward descent, they reached the garden.

They had hardly laid her on the grass when the gate crashed open. Paul, Constable Gordon and three soldiers in Canadian uniforms, crowded in. One of the soldiers had a Red Cross armband. He knelt down next to Rory's mother and checked her pulse.

'She's taken a bad bang that's knocked her unconscious. Best get her to hospital in case there are other injuries. We've got the army ambulance, sir, if that's alright with you? Will you accompany her?'

Hospital? Rory was appalled. That was over twenty-miles away. Rory saw his father glance around, struggling to take it all in.

'Yes, thank you for the offer. Of course I must come with her...'

Just then, Alice, Mum's cleaner, arrived. Rory had forgotten it was wash day.

'Don't you worry, sir,' she called, pushing forward through the crowd of spectators. 'Rory can come home with me and stay over. I'll just pop up and get the missus some things while they put her in the ambulance.'

Two soldiers came with a stretcher. Rory stood helpless as they lifted his mum and took her away.

'It was my fault,' he whispered.

To his surprise he felt his father's arm on his shoulders.

'No, Rory. How could you have made her fall? She was above you.' His father's arm tightened into what might have been a stiff hug. 'Now, be good for Alice. I don't know how long I'll be. Oh, and remember to take your ration book with you.'

The chunky military ambulance, standing outside in the lane, with its big red-cross on the green and black camouflage, looked unreal. It was like something out of a film. Rory heard the doors close. The engine coughed. The wheels crunched on gravel and they were gone.

Left in the garden, Rory suddenly noticed his mother's headscarf on the grass. He picked it up and turned to run after the ambulance, but it was too late. So, he just stood there, twisting it in his hands. It had blood on it. The least I can do is wash it and look after it for her, he thought, before being overcome by a dreadful wave of despair.

Chapter 4

Whilst everyone else in the garden milled around, unsure of what to do next, Constable Gordon and Paul approached Rory. Constable Gordon was Paul's dad. He spoke in a deep, rumbling, but reassuring voice.

'Don't you worry, lad. Hospital's the best place for her. Why don't you come and spend the day with Paul? Alice and I will see to the house. When she's finished, she'll pick you up from our place on her way home.'

'Yes, that would be grand,' said Alice, who had arrived back. She patted Rory's arm. 'Your mum's left the boiler on, the wash won't wait.'

'Come on,' Paul held the garden gate open. With a dazed murmur of thanks to them all, Rory hobbled out, still wobbling from shock.

'She'll be okay,' said Paul. 'You heard the doctor. She's just taken a bang, that's all.'

It was all very well for Paul to try and cheer him up, Rory thought, but he hadn't heard the sound of Mum's head thwacking against the wall, or seen that glazed look in her eyes. Not sure he could trust his voice, he gave Paul a friendly punch on the arm.

'Thanks, mate,' he muttered. After all, Paul had brought the doctor.

'What made her fall?'

'No idea. She was saying something, then there was a

sort of thud and she just tumbled back on top of me.'

'What did she say?'

'I couldn't make it out. She sounded as though she was cross and surprised at the same time.' Rory creased up his eyebrows, trying to think what the words were.

'Maybe she saw something,' Paul suggested. 'You can ask her once she comes round. Till then, let's do something. It's no use worrying. Let's get on with the go-kart like we planned?'

There was nothing else Rory could do for his mum, so he trailed along after Paul into PC Gordon's workshop, where the partly built go-kart took up most of the floor. The axle of the two back pram wheels, rescued from the dump, had already been attached to a long soapbox. This in turn had been nailed to one end of a thick plank, that stuck out in front.

'Where did your dad find the long box? It's just the right size.'

'I dunno,' said Paul, 'but it's great. Look, we can sit one behind the other, no problem.'

'That bottom plank should be strong enough to bear the weight,' Rory said.

'My dad scavenged that from a timber yard,' Paul muttered. He pointed to an ink mark.

'Here's today's job,' he said. 'We've got to drill through

this mark, and this other one on the front axle bar, then bolt them together so we can steer.'

Paul's dad had left a paper plan on the bench with exact measurements and written instructions. Rory glanced at it, but couldn't concentrate. Despair over his mum's accident still clouded everything, dragging at his mind and making it difficult to think straight.

But, as Paul came back from fetching his dad's drill and began positioning the plank, Rory saw what had to be done. Drilling was a job for two hands. He was happy to do it. Leaning hard into the brace, he powered his anxiety down the spinning shaft. It bit into the wood with a satisfactory crunch. Having drilled both crossbar and plank, he stood back. Savouring the fresh smell of sawdust, he shook the tension from his shoulders. Bolting the planks together would be a much simpler job. But no matter how hard he tightened the nuts, the joint still wobbled. The frustration was too much, and in a fit of rage he threw the wrench onto the floor.

Paul tapped his shoulder. 'Hang on, Ginger, let's check the instructions.' He leant over the plan.

'Uh-oh! Guess what? We've forgotten the washers. Mr Campbell would love that. Can't you just hear him, *"Now boys, what have I always told you? Read your instructions."* '

Rory, summoning a grin at Paul's headmaster-mimic, began to feel better. With the washers in place, the wobble firmed up. He gave a few extra turns with the wrench to make sure, and at last, after more than an hour's work, their go-kart was ready to run.

Between them they lugged it out of the workshop and up the slope beside Paul's house. With Rory trying to steer the crossbar with his feet, they let it go. For a few yards it was fine, but then Rory's foot slipped. It slewed across the road, tipped them both harmlessly into the gutter, and lay there with its wheels still spinning in the air. Rory scrambled to his feet and began to right the go-kart. Paul sat on the kerb, rubbing at freshly grazed knuckles.

'What you need for that is a good rope,' called a familiar voice. It was Sven. He must have been watching them from pavement. 'I know where to find some. Hang on while I fetch it for you.' He disappeared around the corner.

'Who's he?' asked Paul.

'He's my friend. He came off that Norwegian boat, *The Kirsten.* It came in after you left yesterday.'

Paul looked up with a quick frown. 'I thought *I* was your friend?'

'Course you are, silly,' Rory said with a smile and explained how Sven had rescued him from Mr Main and replaced his lost fish. 'We walked down to the village afterwards. It was quite fun.'

'Oh. Bully for him! So, did he tell you the great secret?'

'Yes, in a way. There were lots of passengers on the boat. He said they were refugees from Norway. I don't see why they should keep that a dark secret though. You'd think the crew would be showing off how brave they were at escaping the Germans.'

'Maybe that's not the secret,' said Paul. 'I reckon it's something more. You were right. We should go back to the harbour sometime and watch what else they do.'

Sven was back. In his hand he had a hank of rope that ended, to Rory's surprise, in the tufted sally bell-ringers used as a handgrip. Sven must have gone up the tower, Rory thought, but how would he have known the ropes would be there?

'I used to help my young brothers build go-karts back home, when we weren't rock climbing. They were always looking for rope. This one should be long enough.' Sven held up the rope. 'I remembered you telling me about the old bells when we walked back yesterday.'

Of course! So, no mystery. Earlier, Sven had also been at the tower door. Ashamed of his suspicions, Rory thanked him.

'You're always coming to my rescue,' he said.

'Not always, I couldn't find you a doctor. I saw the army medic guys running...'

'They've taken her to hospital,' said Paul, before Rory could answer. 'But it's miles away, so we won't get news till the medics bring back their ambulance.'

'Good news, let's hope. Now let's sort out this go-kart.'

Sven brought out a wicked looking knife and cut the thick sally from the thinner rope. Paul fetched his dad's drill from the shed, so Rory could make holes in the crossbar. Sven then threaded the rope through the holes, securing it using special seaman knots. For a road test, Paul hauled it up the brae, jumped on and tried out the steering by weaving from side to side down the slope, to help himself gather speed.

'Brilliant,' he cried, using his feet to slow down so Rory could have a turn.

'Now,' said Sven, after they'd both had a go, 'I think you probably have the best go-kart in town. Where do you keep it? You don't want other boys taking it off you, do you?'

'Nah, don't think they'd dare. I'll just put it in the shed. Dad screwed in some good strong hooks for it to hang on, out of the way, up on the wall.'

'Anyway, you boys have fun. I'll be off. Don't worry, Rory, I'm not forgetting about us going climbing together.

I'll be back in touch when I've fixed a few things.'

'What's this about climbing?' said Paul, before Sven turned to go.

'Sven liked the look of our cliffs at the headland. Said they looked good to climb and asked if I fancied doing it with him.'

'Cor, that sounds great,' said Paul to Sven. 'Can I come?'

There was an awkward pause, before Sven replied, 'Could you manage with your arm?'

'Course he could!' Rory rushed to Paul's defence, 'You should see him up and down trees and fences. He's an ace climber!'

'OK, we'll see how it goes. I'll get back to you both once I've settled in.' With a wave, Sven walked off towards the harbour.

'See,' said Rory. 'He's a really nice bloke. He wasn't helping just me, was he? He was helping both of us.'

'How about we try the slope from the top of Hart Hill?' said Paul, deliberately ignoring Rory's comment.

It was a long haul, but the sky was blue, and the gorse bushes – covered in golden flowers – smelled of coconut. Far out to sea, near the horizon, a few boats made their way to the fishing grounds, tiny insects on a pond.

'Not Norwegians, I think.' said Paul. 'Even from

here you'd see that white stripe they have around their gunwales. How far out do you think they are?'

'A mile? Two miles? Sven would know,' said Rory. 'He's a useful guy to have around.'

'Oh, stop going on about him.' Paul gave an irritated tug on the go-kart rope, as they reached a place where the path flattened out. 'I'm just wondering why he bothered with us?'

'He only came yesterday. Maybe he hasn't made any friends yet,' replied Rory, more interested in getting the go-kart wheels aligned, ready for take-off.

'Huh,' muttered Paul, 'but still, he doesn't need to go stealing my friend.'

'Stop yakking on about him, will you? Jump in, and I'll give us a push!'

'Yeah! Let's get going.' Paul scrambled aboard and with a whoop they launched themselves off down the hill.

The ride was truly terrifying. Rory could feel Paul clinging to him with his good arm, shrieking and whooping with glee. The wheels coped with the bumps, but the kart vibrated and juddered as it charged over the turf. The slope became steeper. They gathered more speed. Paul's yells were swept away by the rushing wind. Rory found himself yelling too as they hurtled on down.

'Here we come, racing in Queen Boudicca's chariot,

outrunning the Roman guards!'

'Let's win for the Britons,' cheered Paul.

'My arms are coming out of their sockets!' Rory panted. 'The rope's burning my hands!'

He prayed they'd get all the way down the brae without turning over. Skidding to a stop outside Paul's house, they both tumbled off in a breathless giggling heap of delight. Rory offered to let Paul steer next time, but he only laughed, 'I'm alright on a short bit of brae, but I'd need two good arms to control it coming down that hill. No, chum, I'm quite happy for you to be the one in front.'

They'd picked up the rope to start the great haul back up the hill, for another heart-in-mouth run, when Paul's mother called them in for lunch. Food being the high point of Paul's day, he immediately dropped the rope, scooting off indoors. Amused as he was, Rory couldn't help but feel a terrible pang, deep within his chest. He imagined his own mother, calling them in for lunch. Would she ever be able to do that again? Despondent, he dumped the rope by the front door.

Chapter 5

There was still no news from the hospital, and Rory didn't have much of an appetite. He pushed his helping of cottage pie around his plate absentmindedly. Thinking about his mum made each mouthful stick, like eating stones. Blackberries and cream proved less of a problem. When he and Paul had finished they were excused to go back out and play on the go-kart.

After a few more downhill runs they were exhausted. They rested on the pavement. Rory lay flat on his back, listening to Paul's terrible jokes.

'What's a crocodile's favourite game?'

'Dunno,' he grunted.

'Snap!'

Rory sighed, as Paul tried another. 'What's the best thing to put in a pie?'

'Dunno.'

'Your teeth!'

'Oh come on, those are ancient,' said Rory, rousing himself at last. 'How about: What always runs along a street?'

'I know, I know! A pavement!' Paul's eyes shone in triumph. 'Actually,' he went on, 'it should be us running along the street, to look for other places where we can run the go-kart. How about we go to the top green and try it out up there?'

As this was the most sensible of Paul's daft ideas, Rory stirred himself.

'And then…' Paul went on to tempt him. '…while we're there we can look down on the harbour and check that Norwegian boat.'

Hooked, Rory was on his feet, picking up his side of the go-kart rope, ready for the long pull up through town.

After the excitement of Hart Hill, the slopes on the top green were too mild for Paul, so they drifted over to lie on the grassy edge of the hill overlooking the harbour. Most of the fishing boats were at sea, but a few still remained. Among them, moored between two lobster boats, was the Norwegian trawler.

Three fishermen were loading long boxes into the hold.

'What do you think they are, Rory? Not small enough for fish boxes. I do know that. I bet they're guns for the Norwegian Underground.'

'Um…' Rory mumbled. At least Paul's wild imagination lent an air of excitement to their lives. 'It could just as well be harpoons or something else they need for fishing.'

But then a fourth man appeared on deck. He took the lid off an oil drum that stood there, and what he lifted out was unmistakably a gun. They nudged each other and stared. At last Rory was wide awake. The man began to clean the barrel with a cloth, dripping in oil from a can.

'It's a Lewis gun!' said Rory in a breathless whisper. 'I recognise it from the pictures in my war comics.'

'You're right,' said Paul. 'None of these other boats have oil drums on deck. The Norwegians must need that gun in case they get caught in enemy waters. Most of these other boats are registered to Inverness. They'll be inland fishers that don't go too far out.'

'Looks as though *The Kirsten* is getting ready to go back again...' said Rory, somewhat disappointedly.

'See,' said Paul, punching Rory's arm. 'I bet I *was* right and these boxes *are* full of guns for their resistance.'

The men were now closing up the hold. The other man with the oil can was banging the lid back on with a hammer. It looked as though they were finished for the day. All four men jumped down onto the quay and walked off. Other moored boats moved gently on the swell. Somewhere, something metal tinkled faintly against a mast.

'So!' cried Paul, rolling onto his back in the grass. 'Our wee village on the Moray Firth is not just a boring backwater, but an important place involved in secret work for the war effort! Just think, we might be able to do something towards it too, if we keep our eyes open. Who knows, a spy could have seen what we've just seen, and be reporting it to the enemy! Your great friend Sven, for example. My dad said most of the other refugees from last night have moved on. So, what's he still doing here?'

'I don't know. He said he'd arranged to meet someone in the forces' cafe, so maybe he already knows someone in the village. Anyway, what's got into you? He wouldn't need to watch the boat. He came in on it, so he'd already know about the gun and all that.'

'Ah, but maybe what's worth watching is what they're taking back out. I bet these boxes would be worth checking on.' Paul sat up and scanned the harbour.

'Well, I can't see Sven or anyone else watching down there,' said Rory, getting to his feet and looking around. 'Not hereabouts,' he added, as he looked down the hill. 'But there, by your house, I think that might be Alice come to pick me up, so we'd best get back.'

'Oh,' said Paul, 'that's a shame. I thought we could take the go-kart down Harbour Lane while we're here.'

Rory gave a shout of laughter, 'And end up in the water? Don't be daft!'

'Well, since you're such a wet blanket, never mind. I'll maybe come back one day and give it a try by myself.'

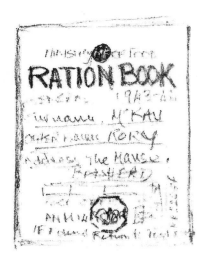

'Never mind, chum,' said Rory to cheer him up, 'there's enough slope here on the high street for us to have a good clear ride all the way down. Hi there, Boudicca, here we come!'

Alice laughed as she watched the go-kart rattle past her and skid to a stop by Paul's front door. She'd brought a bag with Rory's things. On top of the bag was the ration book, which reminded Rory of the fish.

'There's some herring in our larder, Alice. They might go off if they're not eaten tonight. Could you use them?'

Alice looked pleased, so he nipped back home to fetch them. There they were, laid out on a plate, not only cleaned, but beheaded, and rolled in oatmeal ready for the pan.

'My, that's marvellous Rory, they'll be just right for the boys' supper.'

The boys...? Rory's eyes widened. His head spun. Alice, of course, now he remembered. Her name was Alice Munro. There were not many Munro families in the village. Alice was so nice; surely, oh surely, she couldn't be mum to Charlie Munro, the school bully? Rory's insides shrank from memories of books tipped from his bag, sandwiches spat on, and sneaky 'accidents' in the school corridor. And now, he was going straight into the lion's den. He felt a familiar wave of despair.

Chapter 6

It was Charlie Munro's house, alright, and that was not all. Next to Charlie, blocking the doorway when they arrived, was an older brother. Black with dust from his job on the coal cart, he had hunched shoulders and heavy eyebrows, just like Charlie, and an even nastier tongue.

'Och, dearie me, what have we here? If it isn't the wee Holy Joe, lah-di-dah, Rory, from Edinburgh, come to visit in a council house.'

Rory looked around, puzzled. Alice's council house was spotless. If anything, it was more welcoming than the Manse, with its cold, high ceilinged rooms.

'Haud yer whisht, Dougie!' said Alice. 'The wee laddie's mum's just had an accident. He'll only be here for a night or two, till the minister comes back from the hospital.'

Rory was surprised to hear Alice lapse into Scottish dialect. At the Manse she always spoke so correctly. Her sons stood back as she brought Rory into a cosy lounge-cum-dining room. She pulled out a chair for him.

'Sit yoursels to table. Rory's mum has sent fish for tea so you should be grateful.'

She bustled off into the kitchen to cook the fish.

'Feedin' the poor noo, is she your mum?' Dougie's sneer was raw.

Rory shot to his feet so fast his chair tipped over.

'It's nothing to do with her. *I* got the fish and *I* gave them to your mother. I probably wouldn't have if I'd known you'd be here!'

Dougie looked startled, as if no one ever talked back to him.

'Okay, okay, keep your hair on!' His response was quite mild. Rory, still shaking with surprise at his own outburst, turned to pick up his chair, only to find that Charlie had already placed it so he could sit beside him.

'Fishing were you? Was it flukes you got?' Charlie sounded interested, but Rory, worried he'd laugh at him for losing his catch, just said, 'No, some herring from the Norwegian boat.'

While Alice rushed back in, setting down cutlery,

salt and pepper, margarine, and bread, Dougie sat down opposite them.

'Gey funny lot, they Norwegians. One of them had me leave a sack of coal for him at the back door of the canteen. Ye ken they dinna just go fishin'. They sail the whole way to Norway – 500 miles across the North Sea, even in storms. Who knows what they're doin' over there.'

'They're going to help their people against the Nazis,' said Rory, resenting the implication that the Norwegians might be up to something. More so, now that he had met and befriended one of them.

'Aye, that's what's been put about,' said Dougie, 'but what if they're over here to spy on what's going on in Britain? Not all Norwegians are against the Germans. Have ye no heard o' that guy Quisling? A Norwegian himself and now up there with the Germans, smart as you like.'

'Well, I know our lot *have* saved refugees from the Nazis, so they can't all be bad,' Rory insisted.

A wonderful smell of fried fish accompanied Alice, as she brought the sizzling pan to the table.

'Whisht now, and have your tea. Mind yourselves while I serve up.'

Dougie sat back, allowing Alice to slide a whole, beautifully crisp-fried herring onto each of their plates before returning to the kitchen. Rory was puzzled. Had she not kept a portion of fish for herself? He waited for her to return, and for Grace to be said, before starting to eat. Dougie however, was already at it, stuffing in great mouthfuls of fish. Charlie, watching Rory, also hesitated before eating.

'D'ye no want yours then?' asked Dougie, seeing that Charlie had not yet begun. Without warning, he reached over with his fork, hooked Charlie's fish onto his own plate, and began to eat that too.

Rory stared, frozen in disbelief. Boiling with anger, he cut his own fish in two. Giving Charlie a nudge, he slid one of the halves onto Charlie's plate.

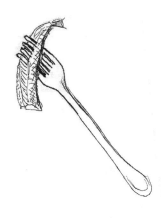

'Oh my, Charlie. Sucking up to the wee visitor? But ye're no goin' to tell Mum are ye?' In a quick snatch across the table Dougie gripped Charlie by the wrist. Rory winced to see tears come into Charlie's eyes.

'He won't, but I might!' Rory said, hoping his voice sounded strong enough.

Dougie dropped Charlie's wrist in surprise, and was about to turn his attentions on Rory, when Alice ran in to switch on the wireless.

'It's the News. Whisht, you boys, so we can hear it.'

Everyone stopped to listen. Even Dougie paid attention. If the Germans had invaded, this was where they would hear about it. Tonight's main headlines were about some goings on in Italy. Everyone relaxed; all that was far away. The next report, on last night's bombing of English cities brought the war nearer, a raid on Glasgow and Clyde bank nearer still, but it was all still far away from their little corner of north east Scotland.

Rory noticed Charlie guarding his plate with his arm, while hurriedly forking what was left of his fish into his mouth. Taking the hint, Rory got on with eating too.

'Shush!' Alice held up her hand to still their forks. She leant forward to listen more intently.

'Today,' came the serious voice of Alvar Lidell, the BBC Announcer, 'the Royal Navy successfully attacked and disabled the German Warship Tirpitz. For several months now the Tirpitz has posed a grave threat to our Russian convoys. Berthed in a narrow Norwegian fjord it has been inaccessible to attack by our battle ships, but today, at last, our Navy have managed to inflict serious damage by sending in miniature submarines.'

'There lads,' said Alice, rising from her chair to clear the fish plates. 'Your dad's on those Russian convoys. Pray to God he may be a bit safer now.'

She piled up the fish plates and left again for the kitchen.

'See,' said Rory, as the News ended and a comedy programme called, *It's That Man Again,* began. 'Our Norwegian fishing boat could have had something to do with that.'

'Shut yer face, ye wee pest,' snarled Dougie. 'I'm trying to listen to this.'

He reached over, cranked up the sound, and turned his back on them.

Alice came back from the kitchen with the teapot. Under cover of this, Charlie tipped his head, grinned sideways at Rory, and passed him the margarine. This was a surprisingly different Charlie from the one Rory knew from school. Had his present of half a herring brought about the change? Whatever the reason, Rory was not complaining. In what felt like a silence of conspirators, they spread themselves several slices of bread to fill up the empty spaces left by Dougie's theft.

'Want to see my war souvenirs?' said Charlie, wiping the last crumbs from his mouth. 'They're out in the shed.'

As Rory got up, he heard Dougie growl.

'Don't think I've done with you yet, you wee show off. I'd watch ma step if I were you.'

Before Rory could think of a reply, Charlie caught his arm and hustled him outside.

Among his war souvenirs, spent thunder flashes, fins from smoke bombs, and empty Sweet Caporal cigarette packets dropped by Canadian soldiers, Charlie had two spent bullets with flattened ends that looked like metal mushrooms.

'Probably these hit one of the concrete blocks they've got all along the beach to stop enemy tanks,' said Charlie, fondling the lumps of metal with pride. 'Of course, if they'd actually shot a person they'd still be pointed, unless they'd hit bone.'

For Rory, the mention of something hitting bone revived the sickening sound of his mother's head hitting the wall. Suddenly he was desperate to know how she was.

'If the army ambulance is back,' he said, 'they might have news for me. I'll just tell your mum I'm off to find out.'

He made to go into the house, then on a second thought, turned to Charlie. 'You want to come?'

That gift of half a fish had cancelled out a year of ragging. Charlie looked both pleased and surprised. They were about to leave together, when the garden gate squealed open. A soldier, wearing the badge of the Canadian Army Medical Core, came up the path.

'Hello, are you looking for me?' Rory asked. 'I'm Rory Mackay.'

The soldier stopped.

'Ah, yes, I met you this morning. There's a message from your father. Your mother was still unconscious when we left to return the ambulance. They've made her comfortable and expect her to come round quite soon. Your father said he'll ring the police station tonight, about seven, as the lady you're staying with doesn't have a phone. Can you go there to take his call?' He looked at his watch.

'Nearly half six, so you should go soon.'

Rory and Charlie ran all the way. Paul, answering the door, looked taken aback to see his regular tormentor, Charlie, in tandem with Rory.

'My dad sent a message that he'd ring here to talk to me on your phone. Is that okay?'

'Yes, of course. Come in. Dad's in the station office. Go on through...'

Rory saw Paul hesitate to welcome Charlie.

'He's alright,' he said, 'he's not as bad as he seems.'

Paul looked doubtful, but beckoned Charlie in so he could close the door.

'Want to see my war comics while Rory's on the phone?' he said, and they disappeared into Paul's sitting room.

Constable Gordon was at his desk, checking some papers.

'Once you've had your chat, can you tell your dad that I'd like a word too?'

The phone rang. Constable Gordon answered it and then with a nod handed it to Rory. The receiver was heavy and awkward in Rory's hand. He'd only ever used a phone once before, to wish his granny in Lerwick a happy birthday.

'Dad?' His voice trembled. 'How's Mum?'

'She's comfortable.' To his relief his dad's voice was quite clear. 'She hasn't come round yet but the doctors don't think they need do anything but wait. They seem quite sure she'll be fine, but I'd like to be here when she wakes. Are you alright staying on with Alice?'

'Yes, Dad, don't worry about me.'

Dad was still talking.

'Rory, before you went up the tower, did your mum bang into anything, like the corner of a bookcase? The doctors found a heavy bruise on her chest. I don't think it could have been the edge of the bell. They're not hung like that. I can only think a block of wood, or something might have been dislodged?'

Rory frowned, absentmindedly running the telephone cord through his fingers.

'Nothing fell down after her, Dad, and no, she seemed all right before we went up. Will the bruise make her worse?'

'No, no, they were just curious as to what could have caused it.'

'Dad, can you give her my love when she wakes up?' He could hear his voice begin to wobble.

'Yes, of course Rory. Now you be a good boy for Alice. As soon as I can leave your mum, I'll be on the bus home. I'll ring Mr Gordon and he can let Alice know when I'll be back. Till then, be good, and don't forget your prayers.'

As if! thought Rory. 'No, Dad. Mr Gordon asked me to give him the phone when we're done, so I'll get him now, shall I?'

Mr Gordon was waiting by the door. Rory handed him the receiver. He sat down in a huff. His dad only cared enough to tell Alice when he'd be back, not him. *Adults don't think children worry,* he fumed, kicking sulkily at the doormat. *They think all we do is play!* As if he needed a reminder to pray. He'd been praying for Mum almost every minute since it had happened. Even as he and Paul had hurtled down the Hart Hill slope, he'd thought, *If we have an accident, please God, please, take me instead of Mum!*

Sitting there, he found himself becoming even more anxious than before. What bruise were they talking about? Had something hit her? He had heard a thud. If only he could have made out what she'd said before she fell. The telephone tinkled as Mr Gordon put down the receiver. He was frowning.

'Did your father lock the tower before he went off in the ambulance, Rory?'

'No, I saw Mum put the key in her skirt pocket as we went up. If you're going to see what might have made her fall, can I come?'

'No, lad,' said Mr Gordon, sounding more like PC Gordon now. 'One accident's quite enough. You go play with Paul. I see he's gone to get his new go-kart out again.

You've made a good job of that between you.'

You couldn't really beg a policeman to change his mind. Rory trailed round to join the boys in the garden.

'We'd better go back to Alice. She'll probably think it's time for me to go in,' said Rory, when Charlie had finished raving about the go-kart.

Paul walked with them as far as the gate, then with a wave and a 'see you tomorrow' left to go back home.

'How's your mum?' asked Alice, as they came in.

'No change. She hasn't come round.'

Alice came over and gave him a hug, 'Unconscious people sometimes take days to wake up. She's in the best place. Now you come with me and we'll sort out your bed.'

She ushered Rory upstairs, calling back over her shoulder for Charlie to come up too. They were to share a room. Rory wondered how that would turn out.

Rory took his pyjamas to the bathroom and changed there, before he brushed his teeth. That would avoid any snide remarks Charlie might make. But on his return, Charlie still seemed friendly.

'Guess what? Have you heard of the Hart Hill dragon?'

'Course I have, Viking story they say.'

'No, it's true. Tom Lakin and I are going on a hunt for it!'

'Get away! It's a fairytale. Are you going out tomorrow

to see if there's claw marks or something? I can't remember the whole story...'

'Well, way back in Viking times...' started Charlie. Before long Rory felt his eyes starting to close. In his hand, he clutched his mum's scarf, holding it tightly to his chest. As sleep turned to dreams, the scarf became reins. Rory was riding a great dragon, all the way down Hart Hill, over the sea. He twisted and turned through the sky, as Norwegian seaman pointed and gasped, and German fighter planes disappeared in blasts of hot, fiery smoke. Higher and higher they went, higher than any man had gone before. Into the upper reaches of the sky, where the dragon's breath frosted over, and there was nothing but soft pink clouds and rushing air.

Chapter 7

Rory lay very still. Where was he? This wasn't his room. No light leaked in through the blacked-out window, but somehow he knew it was morning. Mum! Despair crushed his chest like a heavy stone. Had she come round? He had to find out. Who would know? He leapt out of bed, sidestepped into the bathroom to throw water on his face, then hurtled down the stairs.

Alice was pouring oatmeal into a porridge pan of salted water.

'My, but you're an early riser, Rory,' she said, 'It's only six o'clock. My lads won't be stirring yet.'

'Who could I get to phone the hospital for news of Mum? I don't think they'll speak to children.'

'You could maybe ask Doctor Cameron. He would know the hospital number. He might even be going there today,' she suggested.

'Of course, he'd know. Do you think I might catch him if I go now?'

'You can try. He's probably fast asleep like the rest of the town, but the run will do you good. I'll have porridge ready by the time you get back.'

Rory ran out of the house. The slap of his sandals on the pavement turned him into a Greek soldier, racing as fast as he could to bring news to Athens. The Greek army had defeated the Persians at Marathon, but now, this very minute, the Persians were sailing their warships round the coast to attack Athens. Stopping for a breather by the post office, he became himself again. Make believe was all very well, but his real reason for running was frighteningly real. Mum! With a final gasp he took off again, up the rest of the brae, to the line of houses by the coast guard station.

The doctor's car was still there, parked out in front. Panting, Rory reached for the bell, but the door opened before he had a chance to ring it.

'Goodness me, Rory,' said Mrs Cameron, 'I saw you running. What's happened? Have you come to call out the doctor?'

'Nothing's happened, Mrs Cameron, I just wanted to talk to Dr Cameron before he went off on his rounds.'

'Who is it, Joan?' The doctor appeared, clutching the front of his red dressing gown over his Santa Clause tummy. 'Ah, Rory, come on in, lad.'

Rory followed him into the kitchen.

'How's your mum?'

'That's what I've come about. She's still in the hospital and I wondered if you might be able to phone them for me, to get news. Dad rang me at the Police Station last night but said she still hadn't woken up. I need to know because – because...' He gulped, 'I'm afraid she's died.'

Dr Cameron was suddenly clearing his throat.

'Come through,' he said, opening the door to his consulting room.

Rory recognised the funny medical smell from the time he'd had tonsillitis. A black telephone stood on the desk. Dr Cameron was dialling.

'Pop back to the kitchen, Rory, and ask Mrs Cameron to put on the kettle, there's a good boy.'

Rory left the room, but froze outside the door.

I've been sent out so I don't hear that she's dead.

He clasped his hands tightly together, before walking into the kitchen, full of sadness and mourning.

'Mrs Cameron...please, please can you put on the kettle?' he whispered.

Mrs Cameron looked at him, 'You poor thing, what's wrong?!'

Before Rory could answer, there was a shout from Dr Cameron, calling him back. Rory ran back to the office, expecting the worst.

'Right lad, not to worry, she's still with us. Hospital says she's comfortable, breathing well, but still unconscious. The bump on her head is going down so that's good news, but there's probably swelling inside. That's the problem. Once that settles she should begin to wake up.'

Now Rory could picture it, he began to feel better. He slumped into a chair. The outside bump was going down, and then the inside one would follow, and then she'd wake up. He could wait for that.

'Thank you, doctor. Sorry I woke you so early.' He stood up to go.

'I'm glad you did. Come again if you're worried. I'll always have time for you. Will you stay for breakfast?'

'I think Mrs Munro's expecting me back. Thanks again. I feel better now I understand why it's taking so long.'

Doctor Cameron showed him to the door with a smile.

Rory made his way along the brow of the hill above the harbour. He looked out to sea and formed his feelings into the words of a prayer.

'Thank you, God, for keeping her alive. Please God, keep looking after her, make that swelling go down and waken her soon. Amen.'

He dropped his gaze to the harbour. There was a movement among the crossbars under the walkway. Someone was there, but he was too far away to see who it was. What were they doing? Could Paul be right about spies? If so, what was there for a spy to see?

The crew of the Norwegian boat did seem busy. One of them was hanging in a kind of cradle over the side, rubbing at the registration number with a paint brush. Behind the wheelhouse someone else was scrubbing the deck, and on the quay, two more were busy checking the nets. It didn't look as though they were likely to leave any time soon. All the other trawlers had already sailed for the fishing grounds. Nothing else moved around the harbour. He was about to go back down the hill, when he saw whoever had been down on the crossbars climb back up onto the walkway.

'Sven!' Rory ran down the hill to meet him.

'You're an early bird,' Sven greeted him.

'I've been to the doctor's house. Was that you under the pier just now?'

'Under the pier? No, I've just come from the hostel. Maybe it was the Harbour Master fixing barbed wire to stop you fishing there again, eh?' his eyes crinkled, in that way that Rory loved so much. 'Another guy did pass me as I came down the steps. Maybe it was him you saw.'

The Seamen's Hostel was built hard against the cliff face under the hill, unseen from where Rory had been standing. It was true. He wouldn't have seen the other man if he'd walked past the hostel down there.

'Oh, well never mind that, you should have seen our go-kart the other day,' he said, jogging along beside Sven as they came round onto the high street. 'When you left we towed it all the way up Hart Hill and nearly killed ourselves on the run back down. Smashing it was. Maybe we'll do it again today.'

'Glad it's working so well,' said Sven, stopping by the post office. 'I'm waiting here for the bus that brings the newspapers. How's your mum?'

Rory could feel his shoulders slump. 'Not awake yet. My dad's staying with her till she comes round.'

'Hope that's not too long,' said Sven, patting his shoulder. 'Here's the bus. My friend may be on it. If not, could you keep an eye out, and let me know if you see him?'

'How would I know him?' said Rory, glancing at him in surprise.

'Oh, he has very wild grey hair,' Sven said, demonstrating with his fingers. 'He's like no one in this village. I think you would notice him if he came here.'

'There's no one I can think of who looks like that,' said Rory. 'Mr Campbell, the headmaster, has grey hair but I wouldn't say it was wild. Still, I'll keep a look out.'

The arrival of the bus brought a crowd of people out from the post office. Rory was surprised to see Charlie among them.

'Hey Charlie, you're up early,' he said, catching him up. Charlie acknowledged him, whilst picking up a newspaper from a nearby bundle.

'I came for Dougie's paper. Hang on a minute till I pay, and we can walk back together,' he said.

Good, thought Rory, *we're still on friendly terms.* Charlie took an age coming out of the shop, but when he did come he was bursting with news.

'Guess what?' he said, taking Rory's arm. 'My pal, Tom Lakin, was in the post office and he said he's *seen* the Hart Hill dragon.'

Rory stared at him in disbelief.

'No, really,' protested Charlie, 'he was up with a toothache in the middle of the night and out the window he saw it in the moonlight, flying down Hart Hill close to the ground, with black wings streaming out behind it.'

'Was it breathing fire?'

'He didn't say, but what else could it be, in the middle of the night, in the blackout?'

'Are you off out to look for it today, then?' Rory asked, as they came to the Gordons' house, and saw Paul going out to the shed.

'Come to see the go-kart again?' Paul asked, and led them through the garden. He pulled the shed door open. then stopped. The go-kart was on the floor, not hung from the hooks that had been specially screwed into place.

'Someone's had it out.' Paul clenched his fist. 'Was it you, Charlie Munro?'

Charlie's face went red. Rory could see he was upset.

'No, I never! It wasny me!' He shouted at them. 'Ye

can keep yer stupid buggie! You *incomers* are all the same! Always blamin' us.' He took to his heels and ran out of the gate.

'What does he mean: *incomers?*' said Paul.

'It's what the village people call anyone who wasn't born here, especially folks from down south like you from Stirling, and me from Edinburgh. It doesn't help that they think we talk posh.'

'Well,' Paul grunted, defending himself. 'It's usually him and his cronies who cause trouble. I don't know why you're getting so friendly with him. First, that Sven, now Charlie Munro. Am I not enough of a friend for you?'

Rory was taken aback.

'Don't be daft,' he said, 'You'll always be my best mate.'

Paul shut the shed door. Rory could tell that playing on the go-kart had suddenly lost its attraction.

'Maybe today we should just play up the hill in the den,' he suggested.

'Yeah, let's do that,' Paul mumbled.

'Okay.' Rory checked the time by the church clock. 'See you later. I'd better get back now. Alice has porridge waiting.'

Alice's porridge was ready, hot, and bubbling on the paraffin stove. It smelt good. She tipped up the pan and poured some into a bowl for him, while he told her what the doctor had said.

'That's fine Rory. You stay here as long as you like. I'll be out cleaning for Mrs Liddle in the big house. Our hens have been laying well, so I've left you boys a lunch of boiled eggs, spam sandwiches, and apples. You could take yours with you, if you and your friend Paul would like a picnic. In fact, why don't you do that? Our Dougie can be a bit greedy and might not think to leave you your share.'

Just then, a sleepy looking Dougie shambled into the kitchen.

'That ma porridge?' he asked Rory, making to take the bowl from his hand.

'No, Dougie, this is mine. Yours is still in the pan. It'll be hotter than this.' With that he took a spoon from the rack and went to sit at the table.

Dougie joined him with a bowl he'd served himself, managing to slurp some down the side when he'd spooned the porridge from the pan.

'So, have you heard the latest?' he asked.

'You mean about the dragon on Hart Hill?'

'Naw, that's for bairns. Have ye no heard that they're after a spy?'

'A spy? What's here to spy on?'

'Whit d'you ken? Just twa years since three German

spies were dropped off at Port Gordon along oor coast. The two blokes were took but the third, a woman, she ran off. Who knows if she's still lurkin' aroond keepin' an ear oot for what folks are sayin?' Dougie looked as though he enjoyed being a fount of information.

'So why are people talking about there being a spy now?' Rory asked, pouring milk on his porridge.

'Cos Willi Maxwell, oot at his lobster pots last nicht saw lights flash from your church tower. He reckoned it was some bloke wi' an Aldis lamp. It could hae bin one o'they spies wi' a radio transmitters up there. They've got to be high up to receive any messages. And who can get up your church tower?'

'Who would they have been signalling to?' Rory was puzzled.

'A submarine, of course.' He rolled his eyes as if Rory were stupid. 'And who has the key to yon church tower? There's your dad, for one. He could be the spy.'

'My dad? He's a minister. He'd not betray his country doing a thing like that. Why would he?' said Rory, dismayed by Dougie's suggestion.

'Good cover for a spy, being a minister,' Dougie sneered. 'A nice cosy 'reserved occupation' where he doesn't have to join up and fight the enemy like our dad.'

Rory held onto his empty porridge bowl with both

hands. It was all he could do to stop himself from smashing it in Dougie's face.

'My dad wasn't there last night!' he shouted in fury. 'He was at the hospital with my mother.'

Dougie gave an evil grin. 'I got you rattled though, didn't I?'

Rory wrenched his chair back with a crash and went to the kitchen to wash up his bowl. He picked up the promised picnic lunch Alice had left in a paper bag. Dougie followed him into the kitchen, but before he could start on Rory again, there was a knock at the door. It was Jimmy Cooper, the coalman, come for Dougie.

'Coal boat's in this morn. I'll need a hand to harness Old Daisy, then there's deliveries. Everybody's run down their coal ration, so we'd best get started. Is your wee brother around? We'll need all the help we can get.'

'Charlie!' Dougie roared up the stair. 'Get out o' that bed. You're on the coal cart the day.' Then he left, banging the door behind him. Rory heard raised voices from the garden, and then a dishevelled Charlie hurtled into the house and grabbed a hunk of bread from the table. Without a word to Rory, he followed his brother out, slamming the door behind him.

Rory savoured a guilty feeling of relief. Now he needn't ask Charlie to come out with him and Paul. There was no way Paul would have let Charlie into their hideout. With Charlie gone, they could go straight away up to Hart Hill woods. Perhaps a day together on their own would go some way to convincing Paul that he really did think of him as his best friend.

Chapter 8

The over-hanging ridge of Hart Hill was another great lookout spot. Leaning over, Rory and Paul could keep an eye on whoever came along the main road, which ran below. They could check out all the sand dunes, and the smooth curve of the beach beyond. Best of all, they could see far out to sea, all the way to the horizon. The only place you could get a better view, Rory thought, would be from the top of the Forest Fire lookout post. The metal tower, built like a pylon, stood in the trees behind their camp. Not that he and Paul had ever been up there. Someone had removed the bottom ladder, to deter people from trying to climb.

Down here, they could see all they needed for their game. Lying on their stomachs, hidden in the thick heather outside their hut, they lined up their wooden rifles – targeting the fishing boats in the bay. Today's mission was to scatter the invading German fleet, whom they could already see massing in the bay.

'Ack-ack-ack! That Norwegian fishing boat's a German cruiser,' shouted Rory.

'I'm aiming for that Aberdeen drifter. It's a destroyer,' said Paul, curling the stiff fingers of his bad hand round his makeshift trigger. 'Got him!' he cried.

By lunchtime they'd dispatched seven fishing boats, and three of those smaller ones out tending their lobster pots. Spam sandwiches and boiled eggs had disappeared. Apples had been chewed right down to their stalks.

Rory was about to throw his core at a passing bird, when a twig cracked. They froze. In their game, any intruder was an enemy. The sound of boots brushing through tough scratchy heather made them press even closer to the ground. Whoever it was had paused. Had they been seen? No. Footsteps moved on, but stopped again. There was a lot of rustling in the bushes behind them, as though something large was being pulled about. There was a grunt, a clang, then a regular muffled scuff-and-step which seemed to fade without getting any further away.

Paul made a gesture with his hand. Rory, like a wooden puppet, screwed his head round bit by bit, to peer behind him. Through the heather he saw that something had changed. A ladder now stood between the metal legs of the fire tower. The bump and scuff sound had been the footfalls of someone climbing up it. Silently, Rory pointed upwards.

Together, as if given an order, they wriggled, commando style, back through the entrance of their den. Once inside they pulled a dead branch of gorse across the door. They knew from experience that this made them invisible to outsiders, while still letting them see out.

'Who is it?' Paul whispered. 'Do you think there's a

fire in the forest?'

'We'd have smelt smoke, or heard a fire engine, like last time.'

'Shush. He's coming down again.'

Rory held his breath, and strained his ears. A thud. The climber reached the ground; a rustling in the bush, a scrabble and a scratch, the ladder was being pushed back into its hiding place. Finally, footsteps faded. At last, when all he could hear was the sigh of the breeze in the Marram grass, and the twitter of a skylark high in the empty sky, Rory breathed again. Beside him, he felt Paul relax and raise his head. He shuffled up next him, looking out over the edge of the ridge. And there he was, a fair haired man, walking down the hill below.

'Ha,' said Rory. 'It's only Sven.' He laughed with relief, and made to get up and run after him.

'Stop.' Paul grabbed his arm. 'Wait. Think about it. Why'd he come to the tower? How would he have known about the ladder?'

'You're right,' said Rory frowning. 'He only arrived yesterday. But maybe he's got himself a job as a fire warden.'

'We could always go up and see,' said Paul.

'You mean get the ladder out and go up there? Are you mad?'

'Yes. How about it? Come on. It's a dare.'

Rory didn't like to say, 'But what about your arm?' and was glad he hadn't, for even hauling out the heavy ladder didn't seem to bother Paul. Once they'd set it against the tower, Paul was first up. There were four landings. Rory felt queasy. The highest he'd ever been was up the church tower. At least there he'd always had a window ledge between him and the space outside. Today he felt strange, climbing into the unknown.

They were both exhausted by the time they reached the top. Rory could hear Paul panting. He went to the edge of the platform and looked down. The view was dizzying. Rory held tight to the metal railings, thanking God they were there. He swayed dangerously. Up high, the winds were fierce, and threatened to blow him off his feet at any moment.

Paul, however, seemed quite unphased by all of this. He gestured into the distance.

'Look at that!' he shouted into the breeze. 'You can even see into the RAF airfield, beyond the bend of the bay. We might even be able to see that plane from before, with its engine on fire.'

'Oh, yes,' said Rory hardly daring to look. 'I can just about see one or two, but they'll have our one inside a hangar being...' he stopped, looking at Paul. 'What are you doing?'

Paul was mad. Holding on with only one hand, he was leaning right out over the side. 'I'm just checking if our den can be seen from above,' he was saying, then pulling himself back in.

'Nope,' he said with satisfaction. 'He couldn't have seen us.'

'That's good.' Rory was still clutching the rail, glad it wasn't he who'd had to look. The sight of Paul leaning out made his head swim.

'He wasn't up here long,' said Paul, looking round. 'What could he have been doing?'

At that moment, a strong gust of wind swept across the top of the tower. There was a fluttering sound from behind Rory. He turned, only just noticing a large pile of objects in the corner, covered by a waterproof tarpaulin.

'What's that, then?' said Paul, pointing to it.

Rory was glad of an excuse to move away from the edge.

'Well,' he said, lifting the cover from a jumble of bags and boxes. 'This trumpet looking thing has *Fire Warning Siren* written on it. This suitcase type thing...' He crouched to open it. Paul gave a gasp.

'Wow, Rory, that's a radio transmitter. Dad showed me one once.' Paul, eyes wide, was transfixed with glee.

'Well, a fire warden would need one, wouldn't he? You know, to call people and tell them where the fire was?'

Paul prodded what looked like a half-full coal sack, tucked in next to the radio box. Something fell out. It was slightly bigger, but similar in appearance, to a metal pencil case.

'Wonder what's in that?'

Rory prised the lid open. Inside were five long metal things that looked like pencils.

'They don't look too dangerous,' he said, shrugging and shutting the tin.

'Could they be something to fix on the top of a fire extinguisher, do you think?'

'Maybe. Are there any more?'

Paul poked the sack again and another slim box fell to the floor.

'There's loads of them. Why don't I take one and show it to my dad? He'd know what they are. If they're to do with firefighting, I can always put it back.'

'Best put the tarpaulin over it all again. Rain could damage them,' Rory pulled the cover tight and anchored the corners against the wind. 'Shall I carry the tin?' he offered. Paul would need both hands going down, even more than he had coming up.

'Tell you what,' said Paul, 'I'll stuff it down my pullover and tuck that into my belt. Ready?'

Rory lay down on the landing floor and shuffled backwards, searching for the first step. When his feet hung out over emptiness, he started to shake. Even once he'd found the top rung, he still trembled. Grasping the upright, he took a deep breath. It was a ladder, he told himself, just like the one up to the attic at home. He tried to focus his eyes straight ahead. That was better. Hand over hand, he began to climb down. Once he'd gone far enough to get a firm hold, he reached up to guide Paul's feet onto the top rung.

Going down was much worse than going up. Even the tiniest glance down made him giddy. On each landing he had to repeat the same backward foot search for the ladder, and every time was as frightening as the one before. Almost at the bottom, he jumped the last few rungs. Heart thumping, he rolled over onto the grass in utter relief.

'Quick,' said Paul, jumping from the last rung. 'We might still be seen.'

Fumbling in haste, they unhooked the ladder. Staggering under its weight, they pushed it back into the bushes. Only then did they gaze up in disbelief at the tower, and the sheer height they'd just climbed.

'I wonder why they built it like that, with all those landings and short ladders?' said Paul, squinting up at the criss-cross metal struts.

'I reckon it's just an old electricity pylon, and they've replaced the top with a platform and railings. They've put in landings to give the climber a rest,' said Rory, remembering how his legs had trembled.

'Maybe it was just cheaper to use four ordinary short ladders,' said Paul.

'Could be, but it's probably to do with strengthening the shape.' Rory had a vague memory of a school lesson where they'd had to build towers, with triangles of rolled up newspaper.

Rory got to his feet. He gave Paul a hand to help him up. It had been a long day, and Paul's mum would want him back by five

'I don't think you should say anything to your friend Sven, not until I've shown this thing to my dad. We don't really know anything about him. That stuff could be for the fire warden, but it could also be something to do with the war.'

'I'll maybe ask if he's got a job yet,' said Rory. 'If he says he's the new fire warden that'd clear it up. You know they're saying there's a spy about? Dougie Munro had the cheek to say it could be my dad. I nearly bashed him.'

'Your dad? Well that's a laugh for a start.'

Rory was glad Paul found that funny.

'I'll speak to my dad,' Paul promised, and waved cheerio.

Rory often wished his father could be more like Paul's. Mr Gordon helped Paul with things, like building the go-kart. Now Paul was going to talk to him about the metal box they'd found. Rory couldn't imagine what would happen if he were to go into his dad's study with something like that. He'd look up, annoyed, say not to bother him, and then send him away. Now Sven, he was different. He didn't see boys as a nuisance. He seemed happy to talk to them.

Rory wandered along to the Munro's house. Anyone could be a spy, he thought. It was their job to hide their identity. Someone who didn't have a regular nine-to-five job would be well placed to do it. Not that he'd ever consider such a description could fit his dad.

Chapter 9

Rory had almost reached the Munros' gate when suddenly, there was Charlie, beckoning urgently from the side lane.

'Hey, Ginger Nut, want to come and see a secret?' Charlie's eyes gleamed with excitement. The lane led to open fields behind the houses. At the nearest end were stables, a barn, and an open sided shed for carts. Sometimes boys would say they were going there to see the horses. But their real objective was to push aside a loose plank round the back, creep into the barn, and have a lark messing around in the piled-up hay. This time, Charlie's secret was not in the barn. He led Rory on into the cart shed.

'Up here.' Charlie set his foot on a wheel and scrambled up onto the coal cart. Rory followed. Six or seven full undelivered sacks stood open on the cart. Charlie lifted some lumps of coal from the middle one and gestured for

Rory to look inside. Under the coal he saw a glint of silver. It was a large tin, covered in black government arrow-head marks. Charlie tilted it back so they could read the

yellow label: *Ministry of Food. Butter. 7LB.*

'They're on the fiddle. It's black market butter,' Charlie whispered, beginning to replace the lumps of coal in the sack.

'Wow,' said Rory. 'I'm not sure about the black market, but I do know if you're caught you go to prison.'

'Yeah, but everybody wants a bit of under the counter stuff, so I reckon them what buys it are as bad as them what sells.'

'Who do you think is going to get this butter then? Is there a tin in every sack?' Rory was fascinated.

'I don't know,' said Charlie. 'I only glimpsed this one because I tipped it over as we backed the cart into the shed. I didn't know why Jimmy the coal man yelled at me, but I do now.' Charlie grinned. 'It's like that story Mr Campbell told us in class about the smugglers in olden times. So what do you say? Should we be with the smugglers or with the customs men?'

'It's a smashing secret, Charlie. But we'd get an awful bashing from Dougie if he found out we knew. Let's just watch for now. When you go out with the cart, check who gets this sack. Then we can think about what to do.'

'Like spies, you mean?'

'Yes, I suppose that's what we'd be.'

'We can start by washing off all this coal dust at the

outside tap before we go in, otherwise we'll get caught right away.'

'Cor, Charlie, you've got your head screwed on all right. I'd never have thought of that.'

The cold water from the outside tap left them shivery, so before going home it seemed a good idea to warm up. They pushed the loose plank aside and nipped into the barn. Maybe it was the gloom that made it look as though there was more hay than usual. Charlie had already picked up an armful to throw at Rory, when he stopped. Beneath the hay, there were more tins of butter. In fact, the more hay they pushed aside, the more tins they saw. The size of the hoard made Rory quite scared. One or two tins might have been smuggled from a store, but this amount must have taken a gang to bring it in.

'Quick,' he said. 'Cover it up again. Let's go. Whoever put this here will be mad if they knew we'd seen it.'

Once back in the lane, remembering Charlie's warning, they brushed off the last wisps of hay from each other before turning for home.

Alice was in the kitchen, beating eggs for omelettes as they came in the front door. Dougie brought in potatoes from the vegetable patch, for chips, and dumped them by the sink – still covered in earth. Charlie had the job of washing and peeling them, so Rory fetched a second peeler, and joined him at the sink.

Having served out the omelettes and piles of golden chips, tonight Alice sat with them. With his mother at the table, Dougie made no raid on their plates.

'Are you expecting your dad to phone again this evening, Rory?' Alice asked when they'd finished listening to the news.

Rory could have kicked himself. Dad had said he'd ring to let Alice know when he'd be back. Perhaps he'd already rung.

'I'd best go and see,' he said, wretched with guilt at not having thought about his mother for half a day. He made for the door, and then took off down the road to check with PC Gordon.

There was an army truck parked by the police station. Paul came to the door.

'Did Dad ring yet?' Rory panted, breathless from running.

'My dad's busy in the office but no, your dad hasn't rung. It's only half-past-six. But guess what? Someone's only stolen a load of rations, butter and stuff, meant for the RAF camp. They found the lorry this morning among the trees off the high road, up behind where we were on Hart Hill. Just think, if we'd been in our den earlier we could have seen them dump it.'

All of a sudden, there was a deafening roar behind them. A thunderous vibration filled the street. Looking out from the open doorway, Rory could only gawp. Giant tanks, heading up a huge camouflaged convoy of two-ton army trucks, were rumbling towards the village. An officer, wearing headphones, stood in the turret of the first tank, giving orders.

'The invasion!' cried Paul, his eyes starting with fear. 'It's the Germans. They've landed.'

'No.' Rory grabbed his arm, shouting at him over the din. 'Look,' he said, pointing. 'They're wearing khaki uniforms, not grey. They're ours.'

The tanks rumbling past shook the house, rattled the windows, and then rolled on, right up the high street. As they advanced, people streamed out of their houses onto the pavement, like ants rushing to defend their nests from marauding moles. Until now, war had been something heard of on the wireless news, or pictured in the paper. Now, it was right on their doorsteps.

Rory saw the tank at the head of the column turn right at the post office. The convoy had come to join the Canadian Army camp.

'Reinforcements,' he said, 'this may not be the invasion, but they must be expecting one, to bring all of this here.'

More tanks poured into town, each one taking up almost the entire width of the road. At first Rory and Paul stood still, awed by their size and power. But, wanting to get a better look, they ran out along the street and trotted beside one of the great metal goliaths. It ground along the road, leaving a blue cloud of choking diesel fumes in its wake. Its clattering caterpillar tracks clacked around, and despite being deafened by them, Rory ran even closer to watch the turn of the huge wheels inside the jointed metal band. The rest of the tank towered above him. Glancing upwards from where he was on the road, he couldn't even see the turret on top. Paul, running ahead of him, looked like a dwarf beside the great thing.

For a minute, Rory stepped back onto the pavement to take it all in, imagining himself as Tank Commander, in charge of the entire convoy. The great guns pointing out from the front of each tank carried an air of authority. He wondered to himself how Hitler's army could ever hope to win against these mighty, imposing machines.

'A big display of arms, huh?' said a familiar voice. 'That should reassure your people.'

Rory turned, slightly startled. Sven was sitting on the wall behind him, in his navy sweater. He was smoking. Rory jumped up to sit beside him.

'These tanks are brilliant,' he said, bursting with enthusiasm.

'This one passing now is a Valiant. The next one though, is interesting. It's new, a Firefly, built on a Sherman V chassis.' Sven gestured at it with his cigarette.

'Wow, you know about tanks, Sven.' Rory was impressed

'Well, I trained as an engineer,' he replied, giving the detail of the Sherman tank a close inspection as it passed.

'Do you have a job now?' asked Paul, who'd come over to join them.

'Not yet, I'm just here till I get my papers. I hear you rode the go-kart down from Hart Hill? Maybe one day I'll join you and we can have a go together.'

'Do you think it would carry your weight?'

'Oh yes, and more, I can assure you.' And for some reason, he grinned. Curious, Rory was about to ask how he could be so sure, when Paul prodded him in the back and pointed back down the road.

'I think that's my dad, waving for us to come back. Sorry, Sven, we've got to go.'

'Do you know what I think?' said Paul as they ran. 'I wouldn't be surprised if it was your Sven who borrowed our go-kart the other night. Maybe he even used it to haul all that equipment up to the tower. And...' he added, warming to his theory, '...as you heard, he hasn't got a job, so he's not a fire warden.'

Rory would have liked to stop and argue, but Constable Gordon had his hand to his ear, miming a telephone call. Suddenly, anxiety about his mother filled Rory's head, emptying it of everything else. How would he cope, if his worst fears were confirmed?

Chapter 10

The black telephone receiver lay there, waiting for Rory to pick up. His fingers trembled as he reached for it. To his surprise and delight, his father sounded quite cheery.

'How are you, Rory? Getting on alright?'

'Yes, but Dad...' He swallowed anxiously. 'I'm worried about Mum. How is she?'

'Oh, she's fine – I mean – ' he gave what sounded like a cough and a splutter before continuing. 'She's looking so much better. Only seems to be sleeping. I had a word with Dr Cameron. He's coming over to the hospital tomorrow. He says he'll give you a lift so you can come and see her for yourself.'

'Oh, I'd love that. Can I bring her anything?' Rory could feel himself beginning to smile.

It sounded as though his father had turned from the phone to talk to someone else, his voice became distant. Maybe he was asking a nurse. Then, louder, Dad said, 'Mum's dressing gown and slippers would be useful...so they're ready for her when she gets up.'

'Okay. I'll go and fetch them this evening. Are you staying over there tonight?'

'Dr Cameron will bring me back with you tomorrow, so I'm there for Sunday service. With any luck Mum will have woken by then. Constable Gordon was telling me you've got a convoy of tanks in town. You boys must be excited.'

'Yes, Paul and I were just watching them arrive.' Rory hesitated, then said, 'Dad, why are they here? Are we going to be invaded?'

'I don't think you need worry.' Dad's voice sounded confident. 'Most of the fighting near Britain is happening in France and Belgium. Why would the Germans try to invade the North of Scotland, when they could just cross the English Channel? The Nazis will want to take London, and that's nearer to France than it is to us up here.'

'I was just a bit worried...'

'Well, don't be. I look forward to seeing you tomorrow, and then I'll be home with you. Whatever happens, we'll face it together.'

And with another reminder for Rory to keep saying his prayers, his father rang off. Rory sat for a minute, the receiver still cradled in his hand. *'Whatever happens we'll face it together...'* Had his dad really said that?

He could feel another smile sneak over his face. On top of that, Dad, for some reason, had sounded less worried about Mum. Surely, Rory thought, that must mean she was getting better. It was a puzzle, but at least it had eased some of that doom filled worry that hung over him all the time.

'Better news?' said Constable Gordon, leaning in.

'Yes, Dad sounded much less worried. He says I can visit and bring some of her things from the house. Is the Manse open?'

Constable Gordon took a key from a hook and handed it to him.

'Pop round now, and bring the key back here when you're finished,' he said.

*****

It was a bit odd arriving at the front door of the Manse, like a visitor. The house seemed to echo with emptiness. Mounting the stairs, Rory suppressed a desire to shout out 'Anybody there?' He paused to listen, but there was only the faint rattle of the wind, so he went on up.

Reaching the landing, he stopped to look at the world map on the wall. Every classroom at school had one. Each day, the teacher would move little flags to show where the allied armies were fighting. Tonight, Rory wasn't interested in the flags. Finding Norway on the map, he used his finger and thumb to measure its distance from Scotland. Then, with his finger on France, he measured again. Norway was nearer to Scotland than to England. It would be quite easy for the Germans to invade Britain from there. They could come over in boats. Planes could drop an army of paratroopers. He clenched his hands, twinging with anxiety, but then remembered what Dad had said: *'The Nazis want to take London'*. He checked the distance with his fingers again, and yes, London was miles away. If the Germans wanted to get there from here, he thought, they'd have to fight all the way down through England. Surely, they were not going to do that.

Satisfied, Rory recalled what he'd originally come for – his mother's dressing gown, hung, as usual, on the back of the bedroom door, and her slippers – which were right by the bed. He looked in the cupboard for a bag to put them in. Rummaging around

among the folded blankets, he uncovered a suitcase he'd never seen before. What was that doing there? Suitcases were usually kept in the loft. He popped the locks open and gasped. He was looking down at something he'd seen only this afternoon, up on the tower. Paul had said it was a radio transmitter. This looked a bit bigger and more complicated. Why would his mother be hiding one of these?

More rummaging turned up some dog-eared books. Each page had lists of words. He recognised some as Norwegian, some English, and some that he thought could be German. Across the page from the words were columns of numbers. A code book! Could some spy have sneaked into their house and be using this radio to send messages? A sudden shiver chilled him. If he had called out, the spy might have jumped out on him.

Stuffing the slippers and dressing gown into his mum's knitting bag, he leapt down the stairs. It was difficult to lock the door with such trembling fingers. The key scrabbled about, before finally fitting into the lock. At last it turned. The house was secure. Anyone inside would have to find another way out.

Rory sprinted out the gate, running back towards the police station. He had to tell someone. He slowed and stopped. He leaned on a wall to think. Dougie Munro had said Rory's dad could be the spy. That had been bad enough. But the case had been in his mother's cupboard. Suddenly, a sob caught in his throat. He wanted to be sick. If he told anyone about this, he might be betraying her. Dougie Munro had mentioned that a female spy was missing, and spies could be hanged.

Weary and weak, he walked on, not knowing what to do. Paul's front door was shut. Without knocking, Rory pushed the key through the letterbox and wandered back to Alice's house.

Charlie bounced to the door. 'Did you see the tanks?' he cried, greeting him with shining eyes. 'How great would it be to have a ride on one o' them?'

'Does anyone know what they're here for?' asked Rory.

'They've been called in to seek out the gang that's stolen that RAF food wagon,' said Dougie with his sneering grin. 'I heard some folks won't need their ration books for another year, there's so much stuff being passed around.'

Rory stared at him. Could this be proof that Dougie didn't know about the butter in the bags of coal? Or did he just think that he and Charlie were too young to guess what was going on?

'Even if the black market's not as bad as some think, that gang stole the lorry and they'll get prison if they're caught,' Rory said, looking Dougie in the eye.

'Oh hark at our Wee Holy Joe. Whit d'ye ken aboot anythin'?'

'Time you and Charlie were off to bed,' interrupted Alice, before Rory could respond.

Unfortunately, Dougie hadn't finished. As Rory stood up, Dougie's foot shot out, catching Rory. He stumbled, then fell, landing on his bad knee. The pain was excruciating. He felt his eyes water, then composed himself. He stood up, straight, and looked Dougie in the eye. *No way I'm going to let him think he's scored*, thought Rory. He walked quietly and calmly up the stairs, opened the bedroom door, and threw himself onto the bed. It was too much. Everything in his world was going wrong.

Downstairs, Rory could hear Alice shouting at Dougie. The front door banged. That would be him off down the pub. Rory cringed. Now Dougie would be even nastier to him.

Miserable, he undressed and crawled into bed, pulling the blankets over his head. He tried to say his prayers, but everything was too awful to put into words. After a few hours, he settled into an uncomfortable sleep, with his mother's scarf pressed to his cheek, and a thousand terrible thoughts in the back of his mind.

Chapter 11

Rory's eyes snapped open. In the gloom of the blacked-out bedroom, he sensed someone. A beery smell engulfed him. Dougie was at his bedside. Rory shrank against the headboard, clutching the covers up around his chest. Dougie lunged. With a huge tug, he stripped the bed, and threw the blankets on the floor.

'My Ma does your washing. She says you wet the bed.' His words were slurred. Was he drunk? 'Here y'are then.' A splash of water hit the floor. 'Oh, dear,' came Dougie's mocking voice. 'And now you've done it again!'

More water splashed. The cold drops ran down Rory's face. Ugh! He could taste it. It was only water, but the bed was drenched. Terrified, he rolled off the other side onto the floor, and scrambled under Charlie's bed. Would Dougie search for him? What else might he do to him? Rory pressed himself back against the wall.

Still on the other side of Rory's bed, Dougie burped. He gave a drunken chuckle. The bed juddered as he steadied himself on the damp mattress. Rory heard him curse. He'd tripped on the pile of blankets. To Rory's relief he heard Dougie stagger from the room. Cringing into his corner, Rory strained his ears, willing Dougie's footsteps to continue their shambling way along the landing. They did. A knob turned. A bedroom door closed. He was gone.

Rory shivered in panic. His breath came in ragged

gasps. What if Dougie came back? He needed to get away, but where could he go? If only he'd kept the key to the Manse. Then, all of a sudden, it came to him – the den! It was perfect. There, even if Dougie threatened Charlie, he'd not be able to tell him where it was. Poor Charlie, just as well for him he'd snored through all of this. Awake, he'd probably have been soaked in water too.

Desperate not to wake anyone up, he struggled to pull his jumper and trousers over his pyjamas. He fumbled in the dark, trying to tie his shoe laces together. Wearing them around his neck would leave his hands free. He stopped to listen. Two distant clunks, one after another. Could that be Dougie kicking off his boots? On hands and knees, he crawled from the room, along the landing, and on past Dougie's door.

At the top of the stairs, he stood up. Which steps creaked? In agony, he held his breath, testing each step as he went down, before easing his weight onto it. At last, in the hall, he stood to listen. No sound from the house. And then he was out, safe, into the dark night.

Blackout in war time really meant what it said. No streetlights, no lighted windows, and tonight, not even a moon. No blackness could be blacker. He stood for a moment trying to focus his eyes. Above, there was a scatter of stars, but down here on the ground everything was shrouded in deep, sooty darkness. But the air was fresh, and he knew that the path led to the gate. He caught the scent from Alice's lavender bush to the left. He could find his way from memory.

On the door step, he struggled to untie his laces. Frustrated, he was about to snap them, when the knot came undone. At last, shoes on, he was ready to leave. Arms extended, he felt his way, step-by-step, down the path towards the gate. Yes, here it was. His hand found the top bar. Remembering how it squeaked, he pulled himself up and over.

Shuffling to the kerb, Rory took a step into the road. Now he had tarmac under his feet. Keeping to the middle of the road would help him find the way. Tall trees, in the garden of the big house opposite, added to the shadow, but his eyes were adapting to the dark. On each side he could make out the line of rooftops against the faint glow of starlight. Once he left the village, however, there would be nothing to guide him – only the sound of his own footsteps.

How far had he come? A breeze, sifting through the Marram grass, brought with it the smell of the sea. *I must be by the sand dunes*, he thought. The path to the den turned off somewhere here. The breeze had brought in clouds too, which shrouded the starry brightness of the sky.

Rory's toe stubbed on a grass verge. He yelped in pain,

then bumped into a fence. This was wrong. He'd come too far. Turning back he stretched out his arms again. Yes. Here were the bushes. He stepped off the road to feel for the gap. This wasn't right. Branches of broom gave way to prickly stabbing gorse. As he pulled away, it tore at his jumper. He tried to turn back. Loose sand shifted beneath

his feet. He was slipping, slithering, and tumbling down a steep slope, rolled up in an avalanche of sand that spat him out into some kind of hole. Dazed and utterly defeated, he lay still.

Miserable, he cuffed away a tear. This wasn't the den, but it was somewhere to stay, at least. Under him, a carpet of dry leaves and dead grass crunched and rustled as he moved. He wasn't hurt. Only a few odd scratches along his arms. Once morning came he'd see where he was. If only he'd brought Mum's scarf.

Mum. The thought of her stirred up a sense of jagged confusion again. Surely she couldn't be the spy. It had to be someone else who'd known the Manse was empty. Everyone in the village would have heard of her accident.

Whoever it was had moved in while they were away. But how would they know when his dad was due back? What message would anyone be sending? Nothing happening in this sleepy place would be of interest to the enemy. Tomorrow he'd sort it out. Now, it was time for sleep. He shivered. Even though he was out of the wind, it was cold. He thanked God that he'd worn pyjamas under his clothes. If it got really freezing later, he wondered, would the cold wake him, or would it just keep chilling him, until he became a solid, immovable block of ice?

Chapter 12

It was not cold that woke Rory, but a huge BANG, a blinding flash of light, and an explosion that rocked the ground. The night sky split asunder. Another blast sent a shower of sand spattering over him. A barrage of bangs and flashes roared all

around him. Over the hill, a rattle of rifle fire crackled. Heavy guns growled. Deafened, Rory leapt to his feet. The Germans had come! It was the invasion!

Light, flashing across the sky, turned the grassy crest of the hill into a silhouette. More flashes and starbursts lit the valley where he stood. Now he could see where he must have slipped last night, down the side of a sand dune, in an avalanche of sand that had taken him beneath the *KEEP OUT* fencing.

Grabbing at handfuls of the tough grass, Rory pulled himself up to the top of the dune. Once there, he stopped stock still, and gasped. His mouth fell open in fear. The whole world was whirling up in war. The dawn backdrop showed the sea, black with ships advancing to the shore. Barges were already near the beach. Every minute they were nearer. Farther out, great strings of rockets flew like sparks, from warships as big as castles. Tracer bullets scored the clouds. The sky splintered with silvery flashes that twinkled off the water. Along the horizon, pink-infused explosions blossomed into gigantic golden flowers of light. Around him, above him, and below him, everywhere and everything shook, vibrating and throbbing with noise.

Below the dune, monster barges were beaching. Down their ramps, tanks moved with laborious deliberation, head to tail, like great horned dinosaurs. More barges brought hordes of humans. Swarms of soldiers spilled from them, splashing through the shallows, running up the beach straight towards him.

The invasion, Rory thought. Someone should be ringing our bell. If I'm the only one who knows about it…I must warn everyone.

From the top of the dune, he slithered into the next dip. From here he could see the fence he'd rolled under in the dark. He would dig back under it now, and get to the road. The sand was so soft that it dragged at his feet. It was like trying to run through tar. He paused to catch his breath. A rabbit dashed past him, scared senseless by the noise. There was a loud bang; sand flew everywhere.

'Rory!' His ears were singing, but he thought someone had called him. He looked back. There on the hill, behind him, stood Sven.

'Stay where you are. They've mined the sand. Turn slowly. Now, walk back in your own footprints till you get to me.'

Trembling with shock, Rory made his way back. He followed the footsteps that he'd made on the way down, terrified that every step could be his last. When he came

near, Sven caught him by the arm and dragged him close.

'What are you doing here?' he shouted over the noise of the guns. 'You could be killed. You will still be killed if we don't go. Quick! See my footprints over there? Walk in them till you get to the fence. Hurry, they'll be throwing grenades any minute.'

Sven's angry push sent Rory off on a stumbling run, down the other side of the dune. In the grey dawn light he could see Sven's silky sand-made tracks.

He plunged on towards the fence. Explosions on the shore thundered closer. Reaching the fence, he threw himself to the ground, scrabbling furiously to get underneath. Once through, he pulled himself upright. At least here the ground would not explode beneath his feet. But the enemy had come. He had to warn the town.

Rory hurtled down the road. The deafening bursts of shell fire and thunder flashes cancelled any sound that his feet might have made. It was brighter now. Up here, he saw where he'd gone wrong the night before. From Hart Hill the road had always looked quite straight. Now he could see it actually curved. The verge, where he'd stubbed his toe in the dark, was on the sea side. He'd been misled into the dunes.

He nearly tripped on the kerb by the first house at the edge of the village. The church clock was striking six. The street was empty, but for a boy hurrying towards him. It was Paul.

'Did you get out too?' Paul shouted. 'Have you been down to see them? I thought everyone was told to stay indoors.'

'What are you talking about? The Germans are here. They're on the beaches now,' cried Rory. He tried to run past Paul, desperate to ring the bell, but Paul stuck out an arm and stopped him.

'Where have you been?' Paul shouted. 'Did you not get the warning? It's *our* army. It's only a practise exercise.'

'Our army? *OUR ARMY?*' Bewildered, Rory collapsed against a wall, exhausted. What! *All that panic and fear for nothing.* 'I didn't know,' he stammered, 'I thought it was for real.'

'Wow. You mean you saw it all? Crikey! I wish I'd been with you.'

'Yes, I got lost on the dunes. It's thick with live ammunition, just like they say. I saw a poor rabbit being blown up.'

'Oh Gee. Yuk.' Paul made a face, but recovered quickly and started dancing with impatience. 'Listen, Rory. They're not finished yet. I sneaked out to see what was going on. I thought the best view would be from up the fire tower. How about it? Where were you going just now?'

'I was going to ring the bell for an invasion. I thought

no one knew. Now I feel a right fool.' Rory looked at the ground and kicked the kerb.

'So, are you off back to Alice for your breakfast?'

'No,' said Rory, in despair. 'To tell you the truth, I don't know what to do, or where to go.'

'What happened to Alice?'

'Alice is fine. It's Dougie, Charlie's brother. He tripped me up. Then, in the middle of the night, he came into my room and poured water all over my bed. He's horrible. I'm really scared of him. I ran away. That's how I got lost.'

'Blimey. I've seen him. He looks like a gormless thug. I'd be scared of him too if he took against me. Why don't you come with me for now, up to the tower to watch the attack? We can sort all that out when we come back.'

All this time, Paul had been glancing longingly at the bombardment flashes still shooting across the sky. He pulled a bread roll from his pocket.

'Here, you can't have had breakfast. Eat that as we go along. I grabbed two as I came out. It's maybe covered in pocket fluff but it's better than nothing. Come on, Ginge. Let's go.'

Paul took off and Rory followed, stuffing bits of bread roll into his mouth as he went. What a great friend Paul was. He thought of everything. One day, Rory promised himself, I'll have to find a way to pay him back.

Chapter 13

Despite the terrors of the night, daylight seemed to have given Rory back his energy. Climbing the tower now seemed less daunting. The higher he got, the more exciting it was, as the view spread out before him. All along the curve of the bay barges had come in, but beside them there were other boats that didn't stop when they reached the sand. They just drove on, like jeeps.

'Amphibians!' Paul shouted back to Rory as he climbed. 'They're in my war comics.'

By the time Rory had hauled himself up on to the top platform, the sands were crowded with soldiers, racing up into the dunes between the lines of concrete blocks. From the high point in the tower, he and Paul could see more soldiers, hidden in the dunes, ready to repel those coming up.

As they watched, one of the big tanks raised its gun and fired at a block in the defence line. A thick spray rose into the air. As the cloud of dust dispersed, Rory could see that much of the block still remained.

Along the sands, the chatter of the soldiers' guns reverberated back and forth.

'Their rifles must be firing blanks,' said Paul. 'Surely they'd not kill their own!'

'Of course not. Look, can you see that once the ones coming up the dunes meet the others, they're being sent down to stand with that crowd further along. It's like a game of "Prisoner". Except one day they'll be doing it for real.'

The general noise began to lessen. Only a few flashes still lit the sky. The soldiers waiting in the dunes now drifted back to the sands. In answer to some signal that Rory and Paul could not hear, all the soldiers formed into a column, and began marching down into the town.

Out at sea, even the warships were steaming off into the distance. Teams of soldiers along the shore were refloating the barges, before the ebbing tide could leave them high and dry. The golden sun, calmly rising, laid a sparkling path across the waves. Slowly but surely, the beach emptied, and all excitement drained away.

'I suppose we should go back down,' Rory began, and then stopped, shushing Paul with a finger raised to his lips. The tower had started to tremble. He could hear the thump of feet. Together, they listened. Someone was climbing the ladder. Where could they hide? Rory nudged Paul and pointed at the waterproof tarpaulin. Hopefully it was big enough. Without so much as a whisper, they scrambled under it, huddling together behind bags and boxes.

Under them, the floorboards shook. The climber had arrived. He paused, puffing as he caught his breath. Then came the shuffle of boots and a muffled double bump on the timber. That would be him kneeling down. With a twitch and a rustle, the front half of their tarpaulin cover was thrown back. Something was dragged out across the floor. Rory clenched his teeth to stop them chattering. Paul caught hold of Rory's hand, gripping it tightly.

For a moment, all was quiet. Then came a creaky sound, like a lid being opened, followed by a thin metallic ting – like something being hung out over the rail. This was followed by a quick, almost continuous tapping noise. Rory struggled to think. He'd heard that sound before, but where? Then it came to him – the wireless transmitter! The previous week, "Children's Hour" had included a spy story, where someone sent a signal in Morse code. Under the smelly cover, Rory could have sung for joy. If this was the spy, then his parents were not involved.

The tapping stopped. The boxes were being pushed back against Rory and Paul. Paul's hand trembled, as they were almost squashed. Whatever had been taken out had been shoved back into place. Above them, the cover tightened as it was tucked in and secured. At last, the railings creaked, the floor shook, a footstep clanged on the first ladder. Rung by rung, the climber began his descent. Rory counted his steps. He listened for the pause. At last, once he'd dropped onto the ground, all was quiet. Rory let out a huge sigh.

'Let's just stay where we are,' said Paul. 'If we start going down he might look back and see us. Do you think that was Morse code he was tapping out? I know we learned it at Scouts, but that was too fast for me, I couldn't pick anything up.'

'Even if you could, it would have been in German code,' said Rory. 'Why would someone want to be a spy? If they're British, and they're signalling the Germans, they're against their own country. Why would they do that?'

'Maybe they've got relatives who are being held hostage somewhere, so they're being forced to send reports to keep them alive?'

Rory thanked God that his Norwegian Granny Larsen, his mum's mum, now lived in Shetland and not Norway. There was no way she'd be the hostage. And then he remembered, he'd decided that the spy was the person who had been here just now. But, just as he thought of that, suspicion raised its horrible head again...what about the other radio?

'I bet it was that Sven,' said Paul. 'If it wasn't him, that means there's more than one spy.'

'Do you think it's safe to have a look...if we keep lying down and just peer over?'

Despite his fear of looking over the edge, Rory was

suddenly desperate for it not to be Sven. He was his friend. He had given him the fish, helped them with the go-kart, and last night he had saved his life. He peeked from under the cover. Far below, a man in a blue woollen hat was walking down Hart Hill. Relief! Sven hadn't worn a hat the night before. It might not be Sven after all. The other day it *had* been Sven who'd come up here, but he might easily have been up here for some other reason.

'Did you ask your dad about these pencil things we found?' asked Rory. 'If we could find out what they are, it might explain why Sven was up here the other day. He only popped up quickly. He didn't have time to send any message.'

'No,' said Paul, 'I didn't get a chance. When I got back the Military Police were in with him, talking about the stolen army rations. Then all the tanks came, so I put it down somewhere and forgot all about it.'

'I really don't want it to be Sven,' Rory muttered. 'If we could find out what these things are it might tell us more about why he was up here. Anyway, there is probably someone else. Dougie said someone flashed signals from our church tower. He said they were most likely signalling to a submarine.'

'Ha! Well, I know that's not right, for a start,' said Paul. 'Dad told me our bay isn't deep enough for submarines.

In 1940, three German spies were dropped by flying boat at Port Gordon just along the coast. They'd have brought them in by submarine if they could.'

'Yeah,' said Rory. 'Dougie Munro told me about them too.'

'Yes, they caught two of them but a third one, a woman, got away.'

'So, what would the person in the church tower be signalling to?' said Rory, not wanting to discuss women spies.

'Hang on,' said Paul, holding up a finger. 'We're so caught up with spies that we're forgetting the truck that was stolen. It was coming to a store at the RAF station round the bay. Right? You can see the runway from the church tower. Could it not have been the black market men making arrangements for the hijack?'

'You could be right. Charlie said it was a bit like smuggling in the old days. They used lamps to signal with,' said Rory, happy with this change of subject. 'Oh, and with all this stuff that's been happening I forgot to tell you…I know where that gang have hidden their stash.'

'What!?' Paul was fizzing with excitement. 'How could you forget to tell me that! We could be detectives and watch to see who comes for it, and then we can call for my dad.'

Rory laughed as Paul, galvanized by this idea, threw back the tarpaulin and wriggled out.

'Mind you don't bounce over the edge!' he said, 'I'm sure the butter will wait.'

'Let's go,' cried Paul. He was already lying flat, with his legs stretched down to find the top rung. Within a few seconds he had disappeared over the edge, and was climbing down the ladder.

'Dear Lord,' Rory whispered, 'give me the strength to get all the way to the bottom without getting too dizzy.' With that he took a deep breath, and made his way slowly down the ladder.

Chapter 14

It was still early, only half-past-eight in the morning, when they reached the village. A car was parked outside Alice's gate.

'It's Doctor Cameron,' said Rory, remembering. 'He's come to take me to visit Mum. I need to go, Paul. We'll sort out that other stuff once I get back.'

Alice was surprised to see him come in through the front door.

'Where have you been?'

'I'm sorry, Alice. I sneaked out to watch the soldiers.'

'I'm surprised more lads weren't out there watching,' said Dr Cameron, who was sitting at Alice's kitchen table. 'It was a tremendous sight. We could see quite a lot from our house up the brae. If you're ready though, Rory, we should be getting along. I've a clinic in the hospital at ten o'clock.'

'You can't go on an empty stomach,' said Alice. 'I'll make a sandwich for you to take along.'

Rory ran up to fetch his mother's knitting bag, and took the opportunity to remove his pyjamas from underneath his clothes. Coming back downstairs, he looked sheepishly at Alice.

'I'm sorry the room's in such a mess, Alice. Charlie and I had a barney last night.'

'Oh, you boys.' She smiled, flapping at him with her

tea towel. 'It won't be the first time I have to tidy up after you lot. Off you go. I'll see you when you get back.'

'She's so nice,' said Rory, settling into the car seat. 'I feel bad about leaving the room in such a mess.'

'Aye,' said the doctor, putting the car in gear. 'She's a grand lass is our Alice.'

It would be quite a long journey to the hospital, Rory thought, wriggling back into his seat, and beginning to relax for the first time in hours. Then,

just as Doctor Cameron turned the car, he caught sight of Sven. He was talking with Jimmy Cooper, the coal man. They were walking towards the barn.

Rory stared. If Sven was a spy, then it was totally possible that he was involved with the black-market gang too. Then he felt guilty. It wasn't fair to suspect Sven, and besides, there was nothing he could do. Being arrested for black market activities would be far better than if he were caught spying. Everyone knew that spies could be hanged. He let his thoughts drift. His mind wandered, imagining tanks and soldiers and bright lights in the sky. And then, all of a sudden, they were pulling into the hospital car park.

'Sleep well, Rory?' Dr Cameron's voice seemed to come from a distance. 'We're here now.'

Confused, Rory struggled to wake himself.

'Sorry, Doctor, that was rude of me to fall asleep. '

'Not to worry, lad. You'll be more alert when you see your mum. She's in a side ward. I'll come back and find you when I'm finished.'

The hospital had a funny smell. The endless whitewashed corridors echoed. It was a huge building, built like a maze. A doctor accompanied him. They stopped by a closed door. The doctor smiled, and with a nod, walked off down the corridor.

Alone, Rory knocked gently, and waited. No one came. He knocked again. Maybe he was meant to go in. Quietly, he turned the handle and opened the door. The bed was empty, freshly made up. Whoever had been in it, no longer needed it.

'Mum...' His voice trailed off into a wail. He hung there, fingers still curled round the door handle. Was this why the doctor had brought him? Was he here to see her dead body, and say his final goodbyes? But where had they put her? Frantic, he was stepping back out into the passage to find someone, when he heard a voice call, 'Rory!'

There she was, running towards him from the far end of the corridor, fluttering in a white hospital dressing gown. Was it her ghost? No. It really was Mum – awake, and fully alive.

'Darling,' she cried, hugging him to her. 'Your dad and I were in the day room. We must have missed you and Dr Cameron as you came past.'

After the first hug, she held him away from her as though to have a good look at him, before crushing him to her again. He'd have been happy to stay that way forever, squashed against the folds of her hospital robe. But eventually, they had to let go.

'But Mum,' said Rory, completely bewildered. 'You're awake! I thought you were still unconscious. When did you recover?'

Instead of replying, his mum bit her lip. For some reason, she looked guilty.

'Come, sit in the day room,' she said, taking him by the hand. 'We've lots of explaining to do. I'm so sorry, but we've had to keep you in the dark.'

'In the dark?' Rory frowned, wondering what was going on. Dad was sitting in a chair in the day room. He stood up, and gave Rory a wave and a stilted smile, that didn't entirely ease the tension. Then he pulled out a chair, so Rory could sit next to Mum. His father had never done anything like that for him before. Rory was puzzled. Both parents looked uncomfortable. Were they about to tell him that Mum was terribly ill, even though she was now awake?

'I woke,' Mum said, 'the same day that I fell.'

'What? Why didn't you tell me?'

'We were afraid to let anyone know,' she continued. 'You see, a man hit me with a lump of wood, then pushed me down those stairs. He was trying to kill me. If he'd known I survived, he'd have come here and tried it again.'

Rory leaned forward in his chair, trying to take it all in.

'So you didn't just fall. There *was* someone up there,' he said, at last. 'I thought I heard you speaking, but I couldn't make out what you'd said.'

'That's because I was speaking Norwegian. I said: *"Hva er det du har der"*, that means: *"What have you got there?"* You see, I recognised him. I knew him from my time at university in Oslo. He was one of the student agitators supporting this man Quizling, who now works for the Nazis.'

Rory stared at her.

'In the tower I saw he was about to use a suitcase radio. He'd gone up there to send a signal, probably because high places give the best reception. He recognised me, grabbed a broken beam, and knocked me back down the stairs.'

'I knew I heard voices,' Rory said.

'He really did mean to kill her,' Dad said. 'But we needed him to think that Mum might die from her injuries, so that he wouldn't risk coming here and finishing the job. And we needed to keep him in the village...so we could track his signals.'

'It's Sven, isn't it?' said Rory sadly. 'Paul was quite sure he was a spy, but I liked him. He's been my friend and he's been good to me...'

'You were a great help, darling,' said Mum, squeezing his hand. 'We had news that he'd befriended you. You being so upset really convinced him I was still in a coma.'

Rory remembered his frantic run to the doctor for news. He stared at his mother. She had used him. He pulled his hand away, not knowing if he'd ever want her to touch him again.

And then he saw tears in her eyes.

'I'm so sorry, darling.'

She was actually weeping.

'It's this war. Sometimes we have to do hurtful things to save lives. And you saved mine. Dad told me Sven came round to the tower entrance door, and you sent him off to fetch a doctor. If you hadn't done that he'd have hit me again, to make it look as though I'd died in the fall.'

Rory's head was spinning.

'But how did Sven get to the foot of the stairs from outside, when he'd been up in the belfry...?' He frowned, trying to picture the scene. Then, in his mind's eye, he saw what must have happened.

'I know!' he said, throwing up his hand. 'He must have swung down to the ground on a bell rope, through the hole in the floor made by the old bell. That's how he knew about the ropes to fetch us one for our go-kart. And that's how he was able to come up behind me when I was on the steps.'

'Rory,' said his dad, leaning forward, 'I am so proud of you. You've been so brave, being left alone with Alice, thinking Mum might die. I'm so sorry I couldn't tell you as soon as she came round.'

Had Dad really said he was proud of him? Rory couldn't believe it. He glanced up, suddenly shy. Their eyes met, and then Dad, stretching over, gathered him into a genuine, man-to-man, hug.

Encouraged by his dad's unusual display of affection, Rory was eager to tell his own news. Perhaps, just for once, Dad might listen to him.

'Paul and I found a radio up the fire tower. We think Sven was using it. But I'm pretty sure there are two spies. I found another radio thing in your cupboard, Mum. It looked like the other spy had been using the Manse while we've all been away.'

Why was Mum laughing? What was so funny?

'Why does anyone ever think they can keep secrets from boys? Our son's a detective!' she said.

'After all he's been through, I think Rory probably deserves to be told, don't you?' Dad was giving her a nod. 'That radio belongs to your mum. Because she speaks Norwegian we've been sent up here from Edinburgh by the Special Operations Executive, to act as liaison officers with the Underground Resistance in Norway. It's one of the reasons the spy tried to kill her. He knew who she was.'

'Oh, wow!' Rory stared at his parents. They were not German spies. They were agents for the Allies, working in secret *against* the enemy. On top of that, he now knew why they'd had to move up north. His worries were being turned on their head. He could almost hear the pieces of the puzzle falling into place. Suddenly, days of anxiety were being replaced by a new, warm wash of pride.

There was a knock on the door. It was a nurse, checking in on Mum, to see if she was okay. While she spoke to his parents, Rory remembered something else that he'd needed to say.

'Sven saw the army exercise last night,' he said urgently, 'and Paul and I heard him send a long message on his radio this morning. That means the Germans will now know all about it.'

He stopped. Once again he was puzzled. Mum and Dad, exchanging glances, seemed rather delighted by this news.

'That's one of the reasons he's not been arrested,' said Dad. 'We want the Germans to think the Allies plan to invade Norway. Why else would the army be practicing up here, so far north? If they believe that, they'll keep their forces tied up in Norway, making it safer for the Allies to invade somewhere else.'

Mum frowned with concern. 'Do you think we'll have to get Rory to sign the Official Secrets Act?'

'No, Greta,' said Dad, putting his hand on Rory's shoulder. 'I trust our son to keep a secret without having to sign a piece of paper. What do you think, Rory?'

'Well, Dad, I won't say a word about you and Mum. The only person I'd likely have told is Paul, and he's so clever he's probably worked it out already, all by himself.'

'Don't you put yourself down, lad. Of the two of you I think Paul is the most likely to go off at half-cock and blurt everything out. You've proved yourself to be pretty resourceful,' said Dad.

Rory wondered if he could deal with this new side to his father, but grinned at him all the same. It was so much to take in…he felt tangled, like one of Alice's wet towels. It was a relief when the nurse came back, with a tray of tea and fresh orange juice.

'Are we all going to go home now?' he asked, having drained his glass. Surely there was no reason for Mum to stay on in hospital, not now she was well.

'Well, no, love,' she said sounding sad. 'When I leave hospital today I'll go and stay with a friend. You see, Sven is still here and a danger to me. People must continue to think I'm really in a coma until I'm safe from him. Dad will come back with you. He needs to be there in case another friend we're expecting arrives, and for Sunday's church service, of course.'

Rory pushed his bottom lip out. He'd so wanted Mum to come home again, and for life to go back to normal. Then he smiled, and mocked himself for being so childish. How could he complain? After all this time, they were treating him like an adult. And he'd be safe in his own bed, without fear of Dougie Munro. He felt a wave of lightheaded joy, spreading from his cheeks to his toes. Finally, things were looking up.

Chapter 15

Doctor Cameron arrived shortly after. He knocked twice, before entering.

'I've just finished my clinic. So, anyone for home?'

Rory and his dad rose to go, and Mum got up to see them off. At first Rory thought it odd that Dr Cameron made no comment about Mum staying behind. Had he known about Sven all along? Had he signed the Official Secrets Act too? He was a doctor, after all. He must have known Mum was awake, when Rory had been so worried. Rory frowned. Here was someone else who'd treated him like a child. But then, on second thought, Dr Cameron had been very nice to him. As Mum had said, nothing these days seemed to work as it should.

'Keep safe,' Mum said. Rory repeated the words back to her. There was new meaning to them now, though, and Rory felt a lump in his throat. When would she be able to come home again? Stupid, stupid tears were threatening, but Dad took his arm.

'That's my boy!' he said. 'Don't you worry! It won't be long before Sven's caught and it's safe for Mum to come back to us'

Rory nearly laughed. *That's my boy!* Never in a month of Sundays had he imagined hearing that. It was like something from a cartoon! He wondered if Dad had said it just to cheer him up. Either way, it had stopped the tears, and Rory was grateful for that.

The journey home didn't take long. Dr Cameron drew up to let Rory out at Alice's gate.

'I'll collect my things then walk home,' he said as he jumped out.

'Don't forget to thank Alice, and tell her I'll pop over soon,' his dad called from the window, as the car pulled away.

Same old Dad! *He hasn't changed all that much*, thought Rory. How could he think I'd forget to thank Alice?

He ran up the path and opened the door. Jimmy the coalman was in the kitchen, chatting to Alice. As Rory came in, she looked up, then quickly flipped a tea towel over something that stood on the table.

'Ah, Rory.' She greeted him in surprise. 'Back so soon? And how did you find your mum?'

For a brief moment, Rory forgot what he'd promised. He was about to blurt out that she was fine, before he suddenly checked himself mid-sentence. He managed to garble the words around, giving some vague description of her condition, but inwardly he was horrified by his mistake. He backed out of the kitchen, muttering about getting his things from upstairs. Why hadn't he thought to have a response ready? Lots of people would be asking

him about Mum, and now he would have to lie.

He came back downstairs with his pyjamas and toothbrush, just as Jimmy Cooper was going out the front door. Alice stood in the kitchen doorway, as though blocking Rory from looking inside.

'Bye, Alice,' he said. 'Thanks for looking after me. I enjoyed it.'

'I think Charlie enjoyed having you here,' she said. Then, as an afterthought, she asked, 'You haven't seen your friend Paul around, have you? I hear he's gone missing.'

'Last I saw of him was this morning, just before I left in the car,' said Rory, 'but I'll call in on his mum on my way home, and check if he's back. Thanks again, Alice. See you soon!'

He sketched a wave and scuttled out of the door. He hadn't wanted to embarrass her, but he'd seen what was on the kitchen table. It was one of the black-market tins of butter. Not that he'd ever say anything to anyone, she was the last person on earth he'd want to get into trouble.

He set off up the street towards Paul's house, but before he got there, Mrs Gordon rushed out.

'Rory! Oh Rory!' she cried, 'Have you seen Paul? He hasn't been home for his breakfast. He must have been watching the army exercise. I'm so afraid he's been hurt.'

'No, no he's not hurt. I saw him about half-past-eight, after it was all over. He's maybe gone off on the go-kart. We could check if it's gone from the shed.'

Mrs Gordon looked relieved, and even more so when they opened the shed to find the go-kart was missing. Rory decided not to tell her about the dare.

'Don't you worry, Mrs Gordon, I'll just drop this stuff off and tell Dad what I'm up to, before I go and look for Paul.'

Rory let himself into the Manse, dumped his pyjamas and toothbrush on the stairs, and made his way to the kitchen. He was starving. In a tin he found some ancient rock buns, old but still edible. He took four, putting two in his pocket for Paul. If he'd missed his breakfast, he'd be starving too by now. It must be something serious to keep Paul, 'first-in-the-queue-for-school-dinners' Gordon, from a meal. Frowning, Rory went to tell his dad he'd be out. Without thinking, he opened the study door, failing to knock.

Dad had two visitors. One was the captain of *The Kirsten*. The other was an older man, with wild looking, grey hair. Rory apologised, and began to retreat, but Dad called him back.

'This is my son, Rory, gentlemen. I'm sure he wouldn't have interrupted us unless it was important.'

'Sorry Dad, I should have knocked, but Mrs Gordon says Paul's gone missing. I just wanted to tell you I'd be out looking for him.'

'That's fine. The Captain, the Professor, and I have nearly finished our business. Off you go. Let's hope you find him.'

I hope so too, thought Rory, coming out into the main road. He looked up the town towards the post office. There were a few people around, but nobody was rushing about, as they would have been if Paul had driven himself into the harbour. No, remembering Paul's excitement about the black market butter, the first place to look was the barn.

Pushing the loose plank aside, he went in.

'Paul?' He whispered into the dusty gloom. No one replied. He was ready to leave when he heard shouting outside the door – which suddenly burst open on its hinges. Rory ducked down behind a hay bale. It was Dougie Munro and Jimmy Cooper. Dougie was on top, about to smash his fist into Jimmy's face.

'Whit were you thinkin,' givin' my mother black market stuff! You'll get her arrested for receiving.'

'Hang on, Dougie, ye big dope. Let me up!' said Jimmy, trying to heave Dougie off him. 'I never meant no harm. Get off me. Nobody's getting arrested.'

'What do you mean nobody? I've seen you with that Norwegian spy. Once they pick him up he'll probably spill the beans about all of you.'

'What do you mean, spy?' Jimmy had managed to sit up.

'Yeah, that fair haired bloke. You must know he's a spy. You had me leave that coal sack for him behind the forces' canteen.'

'How does that make him a spy? I just found that sack on the coal cart with an envelope and a note to leave it there - and a wad of money for my trouble.'

'Well I'm no so daft. I had a keek in and saw a suitcase, opened it and it was one o'them radio transmitters. I figure that makes him a spy.'

'Blimey! I thought he was to do with the black market

gang. He was there on the night we took the lorry. He even helped us bring some of it down in his funny wee go-kart.'

'Maybe *we* should get *him* arrested and if he splits on us then we can say 'well he would accuse us wouldn't he, to get back at us for grassing on him'.'

By this time both men had got up, and were brushing down their clothes. Still discussing how they could trap Sven, they pushed the door shut and went off.

So, thought Rory, that must have been what Tom Lakin saw the other night. Sven had taken his radio from the church belfry up to the fire tower in their go-kart, and then used it to help bring down the butter. He grinned to himself. Paul would be pleased to know that.

Rory ducked out of the barn. Wherever he was, Paul had taken the go-kart with him. Maybe he'd just gone back up Hart Hill, and had an accident coming down on his own. Rory broke into a run. On the hill path he scoured the turf for marks, and checked the verge for crushed heather, where Paul might have swerved off in the go-kart. He got as far as the den.

The dead gorse was still in place, hiding their door. He moved it out of the way.

The go-kart was parked in the corner, tucked neatly at the back.

But there was no sign of Paul.

Chapter 16

Rory backed out of the den. 'Paul?' he shouted, 'Paul?'

There was no reply, but he noticed that the ladder was standing upright, clipped to the tower. *Paul must be up there*, Rory thought. There was nothing for it. He'd have to climb. Even if Paul wasn't there, at least from the top he would have a better view of the surrounding area. He sighed, deeply unhappy about the prospect. Perhaps if he pretended to be Jack climbing a beanstalk, he wouldn't feel so bad. To keep the dizziness at bay, he forced himself to concentrate, and fixed his gaze on each step as it came into view. At last, he reached the edge of the top platform.

Peering up, the first thing he saw was a man's boot. The boot didn't belong to Paul. Paul was sitting on the side of the platform, with a hand over his mouth. The hand, and the boot, belonged to Sven. Sven was looking down at Rory, with a wide grin on his face.

'Ha, ha!' Sven shouted. 'Just as I thought, here comes

my other little playmate. Come on, Rory, before you fall down.'

'I won't fall,' said Rory through clenched teeth, clutching at the ladder's rungs, hating Sven for putting the idea in his head. Heaving himself onto the platform, he made for the other side – out of Sven's grasp.

'What's going on? What are you doing to Paul?'

Sven took his hand from Paul's mouth. To Rory's surprise, Paul said nothing. In fact, his face had a greenish tinge. He just sat, silently, with his body twisted and hurt. When their gaze met, Rory saw fear in his eyes.

'You've tied his arms behind his back. You're hurting his bad arm,' Rory shouted. Rushing over to Paul, he pulled him forward, trying to undo the knots.

Sven shoved him aside.

'Okay, I tie him in front if that's better. I don't want to hurt anyone, but you kids have discovered too much. You aren't getting in the way, not today.'

Paul looked a bit better with his hands tied in front. He was trying to circle his shoulder to ease the pain, but the grimace on his face suggested it was getting worse. Rory began to edge backwards towards the ladder. Everything was going wrong. He'd have to get help.

'So, what's so special about today?' Paul asked, noticing Rory's movement. He turned to Sven, 'What's happening?'

Sven didn't fall for it. In one stride, he grabbed Rory, crushing him against his chest. He reached down and pulled Rory's arms behind his back.

'Get off me!' Rory yelled, lashing out with fierce kicks and trying to wriggle free.

Despite his best efforts, Sven still managed to tie Rory's wrists together. Rory struggled, but it wasn't a fair fight. Sven was huge. Holding him by the back of shirt, Sven marched him across to Paul, pushing him down on the floor.

Furious, Rory twisted round to face Sven.

'What's the matter with you? I thought you were my friend. Why are you doing this?'

'I do not mean you any harm… but I must get on with my mission, without your interference. You know too much, and now Professor Spoil-A-Lot has arrived, I must hurry.'

'Professor who?' asked Rory.

'Huh!' said Sven, bending to pick up a big hank of rope. 'This great professor you British plan to send to Norway.'

He turned to look at them.

'You would like an end to this war? Well, in Norway we are working on a very big terrible bomb. One to wipe out whole countries, not just cities. When you British know we have it, you will agree to stop the fighting before it blows you all up.'

Rory shivered. What had happened to the friendly man who had helped him? The same man who had joked with him about the Nazis, who had offered to help with the go-kart. Rory glowered at Sven. He felt as if he'd bitten into a red apple, only to find it rotten inside. It wasn't only Sven's betrayal that hurt. He felt like such a fool. What a dummy he was. Paul had been right all along.

Sven crossed the platform to look for something under the tarpaulin.

Rory leaned in closer to Paul, 'Let's keep him talking. Maybe we can find out what he's planning to do.'

Paul nodded.

'So,' Rory said loudly to Sven, 'what's this professor got to do with it?'

Sven turned to look at them.

'He's a scientist. You British hope he will tell the Norwegian Resistance how to sabotage our bomb. They already tried once and failed.'

Suddenly, it dawned on Rory. It was the man with wild hair! Dad had called him a professor, but at the same time Rory had thought that he looked more like a headmaster than a resistance fighter. He'd never imagined that he was a scientist. Rory's stomach churned. His father was in

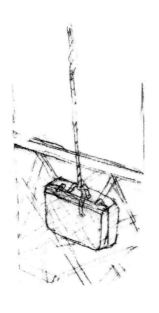

danger too.

Sven pulled the suitcase radio from under the tarpaulin. Then he pushed the sack of pencil shaped objects into the pile, with his foot.

'Tell me,' said Rory, making his voice as strong as possible. 'What makes you think you can stop him?'

'Oh, I stop him all right, because…' Sven was grinning, a really nasty triumphant grin. '…he will not get there.'

Bending down, he passed the rope through the handle of the suitcase, tied it, then began to lower it to the ground far below.

'What do you mean he won't get there?' Paul asked.

Sven stopped lowering for a minute, and turned to face them.

'This boat he goes on, once at sea, will go POUFF!' He waved his free hand in the air. 'And so, no more nosey professor.'

'You're going to blow up *The Kirsten*?' Rory was horrified. He had vivid memories of the rabbit flying through the air. He felt sick. What could they do to stop him?

A rumble filled the sky. Two Wellington bombers roared overhead, on their way back to their base. Rory jerked about, in the vain hope of catching their attention. Sven paused to look over at the RAF base, watching them land.

'And you beauties will be next,' Rory heard him mutter under his breath, before he started lowering again.

The suitcase caught on something as it went down. Sven cursed in Norwegian and yanked at the rope, until it ran free, and finally went slack. The suitcase had reached the ground. Sven cut more rope, to tie around the mouth of the coal sack.

'Oh,' said Paul. 'I thought you'd just chuck that one over the side.'

Sven laughed, 'And blow us all up?'

'What d'you mean?' said Paul. 'They're only cigars.'

Sven was really laughing now.

'Oh, you boys! You had a good look at my things, did you not? No, they're not cigars. They are timers to delay explosions, so I can be far away when my bomb goes off. So, yes, gently, gently I shall lower them down.'

Cripes, thought Rory. Paul had been running around with one in his pocket! He could have ended up just like the rabbit. Rory watched as the sack snagged, but not so much as the suitcase. Sven seemed to have found a better lowering technique. At last, it reached the ground. Dropping the rope over the rail, Sven turned back to them.

'You see, I mean you no harm. Someone will soon come to find you, but I must be sure you stay up here till my job is done.'

He crossed to the ladder, then disappeared over the side. Rory listened to his footfalls until he reached the next landing. The ladder began to jerk. With an ear-splitting crack, the clips holding it to their platform tore from the wood. The ladder jackknifed into the air, before crashing onto the ground below.

'Sorry, boys,' Sven's voice floated up. 'Just making sure you stay there for now.'

Chapter 17

The second Sven left, they kicked into action. Paul pushed himself towards Rory, trying to get at the ropes tying his hands. At Scouts, in games of "prisoner" they'd learned how to keep their wrists stiff whilst being tied up, so that they could later work them out of a rope. Unfortunately, Sven's knots were a bit tighter than the Scout leader's. Paul used his teeth, biting and tearing at the binds. After a good minute, Rory managed to twist one hand free. Paul sat back, spitting out fragments of cord.

Shaking the rope from his other hand, Rory started untying the knots on Paul's wrists. It was a struggle, but once he'd got them undone, he sat back to rub his own. It was only then that he noticed Paul's bad arm. It had flopped back at his side, and hung limp.

'Oh gosh,' Rory gasped, desperate with worry. 'What's Sven done to you? Does it hurt?'

'It only hurts a bit.' Paul's voice was weak. He winced as he tested his arm with his good hand. 'I think that maybe it's out of its socket or something.' He gave a feeble grin. 'It felt better when it was tied up.'

'What if I made you a sling?' asked Rory.

'Oh,' said Paul, 'would you?'

''Course I will. That's what friends are for,' said Rory, pulling off his jumper.

After a bit of jiggling, he tied the jumper round Paul's

neck, and gently settled the limp arm into the loop he'd made.

'Any better?'

Paul nodded. Looking at Rory sheepishly, he said, 'When you arrived I thought you'd side with Sven.'

'How could you possibly think that?' cried Rory in dismay. He looked away. 'I'm sorry. You were right about him all along. I just didn't want to believe you.' Foraging in his pocket, he brought out one of his mother's rock buns. 'Peace offering,' he said. 'I thought you'd be starving when I found you.'

'Cor! Ta, Ginge. I could sure use that!' Paul grinned.

'I'm sorry, chum, I'll have to leave you. I've got to hurry and warn the boat crew about the bomb.' Forgetting that the ladder had gone, he rushed to the platform's edge. The world tipped upside down. His head span, and he stumbled backwards, in a dizzy whirl of sickness. 'The ladder's gone! I'll never get down.'

'Yes, you will,' said Paul. 'Look, he's left all this rope.' He gestured at what was left of the coil by the railing. 'All you have to do is use that to drop down over the edge.'

Over the edge! For the first time that day, Rory felt a stab of real fear. He started sweating. There was no way he was going to do that. One step towards the platform's edge and his leg muscles turned to water. No amount of persuasion from his brain could force him to climb out over the side. Paul's casual use of the word *drop* had been echoed by a lurch of his stomach, as though it had already begun to fall away.

'I can't,' he heard himself whimper.

'So, you're quite happy for all those men to be blown up, are you?'

'I'm height sick,' he protested.

'No, you're not. You got up here!'

'But it was torture. Every time the ladders shook, I cringed. I hate going near the edge.' He glanced towards it again, and felt sick. 'I have to hold on all the time because I get dizzy. I can't go down on a rope. I really can't!'

'Listen,' he continued, clutching at straws. 'Why don't we just get out the fire siren and wind it up? People would hear it and come. Then we can tell them about the bomb.'

'No,' said Paul. 'It'd be ages before they got here. Everyone would mess about wondering whose job it was to respond. They'd think it was a police job and my dad's away at the moment.' Paul glared at Rory. 'You need to get to the harbour much quicker than that. Sven took his radio and stuff, so he must be moving on. I bet he's already got the bomb in place. We need to warn them quick as we can. Stop making your usual fuss about nothing. You're going to have to go over the side – height sickness or not!'

'I can't. I really, really can't,' Rory repeated miserably. Eyes lowered to the floor, he began to shiver. His head was spinning. He and only he would be responsible for the death of all these men, the professor, and that captain who'd smiled at him in his dad's study.

'My dad!' he cried, suddenly remembering. 'He'll be killed too.'

'What's your dad got to do with it?'

'I saw him with the professor at our house, just before I found you. What if my dad goes to the boat with them?'

'Crikey, he'll get blown up.'

'Shut up!' Visions of the rabbit filled his mind again. 'I've got to find a way to get down and save them.' He stared at a slight gap between the floorboards. In a second he was on his knees, peering through it at the platform below. To his surprise, it didn't look very far.

'Hey, Paul,' he cried in excitement, 'if we could prise up one of the floorboards I can get down to the next level on a rope, and continue on the ladders from there.'

'You mean, like that time we let ourselves down from your loft onto the landing? Brilliant.' Paul sounded equally excited. 'Quick now, find something to prise up the plank.'

Rory pulled back the tarpaulin. Amongst the jumble of rubbish, there were some old rags, steel clips, broken boxes and tins. A quick rummage turned up a thin metal bar. That would do. He turned to show Paul, who was now lying flat, peering over the edge. With a dizzy gasp, Rory almost changed his mind. But no, he *could* do it. He was Captain Mackay – a courageous resistance fighter on a special mission to foil the enemy.

'I'm trying to see where we could anchor the rope,' Paul called up to him. 'I can't hang onto it one-handed, and I don't know if the railings will hold your weight.'

Resistance fighters didn't worry about weak ropes. Rory would find a way.

'Come here. Hang onto this post,' Paul called.

Rory took control. He crouched beside Paul.

'Look.' Rory pointed to the corner, where the leg of the tower, the metal struts, and the frame of the platform had been welded together in one lump. 'I can tie the rope round there in a double round turn and two half hitches.'

'I remember the scout master saying an elephant couldn't break out of that knot,' said Paul. 'It should be strong enough to hold a wee runt like you!'

Rory nudged him. 'Who're you calling a runt?' he protested, happy to be back on friendly name-calling terms.

Rolling onto his good arm, Paul looked up at him. 'Aye, maybe you do look a wee bit bigger now.' He smiled, 'What have you got there?'

'I found this bar. Let's see if it'll lift up a plank.'

Choosing a spot near the middle of the platform, Rory dug it between the timbers, praying that it wouldn't make the whole floor disintegrate. To his surprise, one plank came up easily. Looking down through the gap, he could see that, true enough, the landing below was not so very far away. It wouldn't be too difficult to slide down there after all. As resistance fighter Captain Mackay, he could do that. It was certainly much less horrifying than having to go over the edge of the tower.

'Right,' he said, 'let's get going.'

Having tied the metal bar to the rope, he dropped it through the hole in the floor. Pulling it back up, he measured out another length to give himself a double strand.

Paul was curious. 'What you doing that for?'

'One strand held the radio, but if you hadn't noticed, I weigh a bit more than a radio. Even if you do think I'm a wee runt, I'm having two strands.'

Feeling his way rather than looking, he reached the rope end behind a metal strut once, twice, then secured it with four half hitches. He leaned back with all his weight and pulled tight. The post didn't budge.

'Hey, Paul, sift through that junk,' he said. 'See if you can find something for me to wrap around my hands.'

'What do you want that for?' asked Paul, crawling to the tarpaulin.

'I don't want to get rope burns, silly.'

It was time. Captain Mackay sat boldly on the edge of the gap in the floor. Heaving a frantic silent prayer, he pushed himself off.

Chapter 18

Rory plummeted. He fell, roughly, onto the splintery timbers below, tumbling over. For a second he just lay there, relieved to be alive. Nothing seemed to hurt, either.

'You okay?' Paul yelled down through the gap.

Rory scrambled to his feet in triumph. He looked up with a grin. 'Made it! Now for the bomb,' he shouted and headed for the ladder.

To his surprise, Captain Mackay was taking over and calling up to Paul. 'Once I'm down, I'll get the go-kart from the den. At your house I'll take your bike from the shed and might still get to the harbour before Sven.'

The bomb! That's what all this was about. Now it was a race to get to the harbour and warn the crew of the boat. But could he make it? Sven had left ages ago.

He rushed over to the ladder, scrabbling his foot onto the top rung, before slithering and scrambling down to the next level. He was so intent on the mission at hand, that he barely noticed the vibration of the ladder. He jumped the last few steps to the ground, and dashed towards the den.

Sven hadn't said when the boat was due to leave, but Rory knew that the professor was already in the village. It all made sense now. This was the *friend* they'd all been waiting for. A few days ago Dad had said something about a boat not waiting till *their friend* arrived. Sven had asked him to look out for his *friend*. Now that this friend had arrived, the boat would no longer need to wait. It would be ready to leave – and there was every possibility that his father would see his friend onto the boat. *Oh, Dad, don't get blown up, please.*

Yanking the dead gorse bush out of the den's doorway, he stabbed his hand on the prickles.

'Ouch!' He tossed the gorse aside.

Now for the go-kart; a jerk on its rope brought it smoothly out onto the path. He lined up its wheels for the ride down, jumped aboard, and was off. Thank goodness it wasn't raining. In fact, as though nothing could possibly go wrong on such a day, the sun was beaming down on him.

Carrying only one passenger, the go-kart leapt forward. Rory was glad of the rags he'd kept wrapped around his hands, as he strained on the steering rope. In tune with his need to hurry, the wheels seemed to whizz faster. He was leaning right back, using all of his strength to make it run straight, when suddenly, two boys leapt out in front of him from the bushes.

With a snatch at the rope, he skidded sideways to avoid them. Hurtling out of control, the go-kart leapt off the path, and crashed with a wild bounce into the thick heather of the verge.

Oh Lord. It was Charlie and his friend Tom Lakin!

'Out of my way, you idiots!' Rory yelled, jumping out and heaving at the wheels to pull them back onto the track. 'I'm after a spy with a bomb!'

'Oh yeah?' Tom said, mocking him and grabbing kart's rope. 'Well, *we're* after a *dragon!* Give us a lend of your go-kart and we'll get after it quicker.'

'Get off,' Rory snarled, and tugged the rope out of Tom's hand. 'No, mates, I'm serious. I need your help. Paul Gordon's hurt. He's stuck up the fire tower. Could you lot go see if you can get him down?'

'Ger on!' said Charlie in surprise. 'That's where we were going anyway. You mean he's right up at the top? What happened to him?'

'I told you,' said Rory, struggling with the wheels and beckoning for Charlie to help, 'it was that spy, he caught us and twisted Paul's bad arm.'

With one final yank the go-kart was free of the heather. Jumping aboard, Rory pushed off, calling back to them, 'I'm off to stop him doing something much worse.'

The go-kart leapt and bumped on down the hill, warm wind whistled against Rory's ears, and his eyes watered. He whooped as the kart gathered speed and momentum, carrying him all the way to Paul's house. Using his foot as a brake, he skidded to a halt and leapt off. Mrs Gordon rushed out to greet him.

'Rory, did you find Paul?' she cried.

'Yes, he's fine, I found him,' he called and dodged her attempt to grasp his arm, running straight past and towards the shed. 'He's up the fire tower,' he shouted back to her. 'I'm borrowing his bike to go and get help.'

Dragging the bike out, he hopped onto it, praying he'd be forgiven for that white lie. If he'd had to stay and explain everything to her he'd never have got away. He peddled like a mad thing past the Forces' café, but the unfamiliar gears on Paul's bike stalled his progress. Each time he flicked the lever the wretched chain would jump, the bike would shudder, and he'd nearly fall off. By the time he'd got it right he was passing the post office, and then, at last, swooping down Harbour Lane.

Great, *The Kirsten* was still there. But no! On deck, one of the crew was stowing the mooring ropes. She was drawing away from the dockside.

'Stop, Stop! There's a bomb on board,' Rory shouted, still peddling frantically along the quay. No one seemed to hear him. A group of bystanders gave him a look as if to say, 'Huh! Boys and their games!'

Then, suddenly, a man was yelling, lunging towards Rory. It was the harbour master.

"Stop! Stop you little varmint. No cycling on the pier!'

'No, can't stop. Listen, listen to me!' Rory shouted as loud as he could, and made a frenzied swerve past him. 'I've got to stop that boat. There's a bomb on board.'

The trawler had now swung out into the main stream. A white churn of wake swirled from her stern. The bows turned into the main channel, setting *The Kirsten* on course for the harbour mouth. Desperate, Rory peddled along the quay beside it, shouting as he went. A sailor looked up, saw him, but put his hand to his ear and shook his head. The engine noise was drowning Rory's voice.

Up ahead was the high walkway. There was nothing for it – Captain Mackay had to take immediate action. He was off the bike, letting it fall with a crash. He scrabbled down onto the wooden crossbars where they'd fished the other day. There was *The Kirsten*, passing close by. Timing was everything. Rory closed his eyes. He took a long, deep breath...

With all his might, he leapt through the air.

Chapter 19

Rory landed hard. A blinding pain shot up his arm. He lay there, helpless, like a heap of rubbish on the deck. How was he going to convince the crew to take him seriously? Again, he struggled to rise, but the jangle of pain sent him tumbling back against the side of the boat. To his horror, the captain came crashing out of the wheelhouse, roaring like an angry bull. Rory cringed. Now he'd be for it. But at least the engine noise had puttered to a stop.

'You stupid bumpkin! What's this thing you think you're doing?' Red faced, the captain towered over him.

'You've got a bomb on the boat, sir,' Rory called up to him in a weak voice. 'Sven, the man you brought in on Tuesday, is a spy. He's put a bomb on your boat.'

'What nonsense. Where you hear such a story? Why should I believe you? Of course there is no bomb!' The captain tossed his head in exasperation, but then stopped to look back at Rory. 'Didn't I just meet you when I visit your father? What would he have to say about this nonsense?'

'Is my dad on board?' Through gasps of pain, Rory kept on speaking. 'Please, you have to find the bomb.'

A shadow fell across his face. He gazed up, and there was the man with the wild grey hair. *I was right,* he thought, *This boat was waiting for the professor.*

'Captain – ' the professor came forwards. 'You're right, this is the minister's son. I don't think he's likely to lie or be up to mischief.' He looked down at Rory. 'This man, Sven, has he got fair hair?'

When Rory nodded, the professor spun round to face the captain.

'Then that's the man I saw earlier. He came on board and went below, saying he'd left something here when he came in with you three days ago.'

'That's him,' cried Rory, attempting to stand, but slumping onto the deck again.

'Where'd he go?' The captain caught the professor by the arm.

'Up the bow end,' he answered, pointing, 'then down into the hold.'

Somebody yelled in Norwegian. Crewmen dashed past and disappeared below. The wooden boards reverberated under Rory's back, as men thundered around in the hold, frantically searching. Those that remained on deck stood stock still, ears strained, gripped by danger. If there was a bomb, how long before it went off? For a moment there was silence, broken only by the gentle slapping of the waves along the side of the boat.

Gritting his teeth, Rory stared down the engine room steps, willing the hunt to succeed. Then, suddenly, his stomach gave a churn of excitement. Something stirred in a breath of sea breeze. A wisp of blue wool fluttered fitfully, snagged on the splintered edge of a crack between two planks.

'There! There!' he shouted up to the captain, 'There!' With his good hand, he pointed to the strand of wool. 'I saw him wrap the bomb in his blue woollen hat. That's come from it. The bomb could be in behind there.'

The captain shouted in Norwegian, bringing one of the crew rocketing back up on deck. He bent to peer at the break in the planks. With a careful finger, he eased them apart. There it was, the bundle, settled like an egg, cupped in the blue knitted hat. Fascinated, Rory watched as the crewman teased aside the woollen border, to show the cigar type sticks that he and Paul had seen Sven take from under the tarpaulin. They were wired up in a complicated way, to something that looked like a clock.

Despite the pain, Rory instinctively tried to clench his fists. He held his breath as the crewman drew a pair of pliers from his pocket. The man wiped perspiration from his brow as he considered which wire to cut. The tiny sound of a snip clipped the silence, and the whole ship seemed to sag with relief. A shout went up, as the bomb disposal genius stepped back. He'd done it!

Tension released, Rory's felt his shoulders slump, only to feel another sickening stab of pain up his arm.

The professor, turning from where he'd been watching

like everybody else, nearly tripped over Rory's legs.

'What's the matter lad?' he asked in surprise. 'Why are you still lying there? The bomb has been made safe now.'

'Let's get you up,' said the captain, but as soon as Rory moved to reach the outstretched hand, he had to muffle a scream. The entire right side of his body burned.

'Oh, dear, you must have broken something when you fell jumping on board,' said the professor, crouching down beside him. He sounded serious. Worse still, Rory saw him send an anxious glance towards the captain.

Rory turned his head to look at what was worrying them. His arm was still attached to his body, but it was sticking out, unnaturally so, at a very odd angle. *It shouldn't be there,* he thought, *how strange.* He flopped down onto the hard wooden deck – unconscious.

Chapter 20

It was strange to be back at school again after such a week of excitement, and it was even stranger having to manage his schoolbag one-handed. The fall had given him what they called a compound fracture of the elbow. The hospital had not only set his arm at an angle, but they'd also encased it in a thick

heavy plaster and placed it in a sling for support.

One handed, he tried his classroom door, but it was too difficult. In a fit of irritation, he turned his back and bumped it open with his bottom.

'You're learning!' called Paul's voice. Here he was, also wearing a sling, the one handed champion of the world. *Dad might be right,* thought Rory, *Paul could probably teach me a thing or two.*

With a clatter of footsteps, Charlie and Tom arrived to join them.

'Hey, guess what? Now we've got two walking

wounded in class.'

Charlie might have been back to his old tricks, but today the sneer was gone from his voice. Rory knew he was only teasing.

'Cor! That's a great plaster cast you've got there,' said Tom. 'You look like a proper hero. Did you really jump onto a moving boat?'

'Yeah,' said Rory, 'and did you really get Paul back down from the tower?'

Stuck in the hospital, Rory had missed out on the rescue details.

'It was mostly Charlie,' said Tom. 'Paul threw down some of that rope, so we could tie it to the ladder your spy had chucked over the side. It was a hard job, but we managed to pull it back up between us.'

'I thought they'd never manage it,' said Paul. 'I could hear them grunting and pechin' away. But they managed to get it up to the level below me.'

'Then,' added Tom, grinning at Charlie, 'my mate here set it against the gap you'd made, went up and stood halfway to the top. Paul managed a few steps down. He couldn't hold on with his bad hand, so Charlie walked him down the rest of the ladders. You should have seen Charlie holding Paul in front of him, like the meat in a sandwich, all the way down till they got to the ground.'

'Get along you boys.' The headmaster had overtaken them and was making shooing gestures. 'Hurry up, assembly's about to begin and we have important visitors joining us this morning.'

Rory grinned as Charlie held the door open for them. The general chatter in the hall rose by a few decibels as they came in; interesting slings and a plaster of Paris marked them out for attention. Feeling rather exposed, Rory dropped onto the nearest bench.

Once seated, he whispered to Paul, 'Were they able to fix your arm?'

'Yep, it was dislocated, just as I thought. They simply pulled it out and it popped back. Well...not really *simply* pulled it out, I yelled like blue murder.'

'I did too when they were setting mine, but I'd done it to myself, you didn't. I'd like to find Sven and bash his head in,' Rory growled in a low voice.

'You'd have to find him first. He's got clean away,' replied Paul, but then hushed as the headmaster appeared on the stage.

The piano struck up a hymn, and everyone stood.

'Onward Christian Soldiers, Marching as to war.'

We're not just *"marching as to war"* Rory thought, *we're actually in a war.* Just as Mum said, it was the fault of the war that Sven had acted as he did. But Rory couldn't work out why Sven had left him and Paul alive. He'd said he didn't mean them any harm. He'd only hit Mum because she'd found him out. Rory remembered how sincere Sven had sounded, talking of the bomb to end all war. He spoke of it only to be used as a threat, not as something to kill people.

'You want this war to end don't you?' Had Sven really thought he was ending the war? Why had he bothered to help with their go-kart? Why had he saved Rory's life in the dunes?

A final crescendo of chords finished the hymn. Rory fumbled behind him for the bench and sat down. The headmaster was welcoming a group of visitors onto the stage. There was an RAF officer with three stripes on his sleeve, an officer from the Canadian Army wearing his pale khaki uniform, and an official, boring looking man, in a black pinstriped suit.

Rory slumped in his seat. Not another lecture on war shortages, how to use your gasmask, or a warning not to waste paper. He was just drifting off into a daydream, when Paul gave him a shove.

'It's us,' he hissed. 'They want us up on the stage.'

'... thanks to the bravery of these four boys.'

The headmaster waited, while Rory, Paul, Tom and Charlie clumped their way up the steps. Rory stood rather sheepishly in the line, looking out at the rest of the school.

'For bravery, and for averting a terrible disaster, I am empowered in the name of the King and our Government to present these Certificates of Merit to you four boys.'

The man in the pinstriped suit began to hand out the certificates. The school erupted into cheers and applause. As he passed down the line, Rory fumbled with his certificate, whilst at the same time shaking the man's hand. He felt a fool, standing there trying to manage his heavy plaster, not knowing whether to return to his seat or to stay where he was.

The government official had not finished yet. He was still addressing them.

'I have two boys about your age,' he began, 'and I'm sure they'd be pretty unimpressed by a square of paper, even one with a government stamp on it. I have therefore arranged for the kind of thank you I feel you lads would appreciate much more. Wing Commander Flint from the neighbouring air field has agreed, straight after this Assembly, to take you four on a guided tour of the RAF base.'

The whole assembly gave a jealous gasp of surprise, and then another round of applause.

'However, for the rest of the school, I think all of you would like to hear in detail from Captain Trudeau of the

Canadian Bomb Disposal Squad about how they actually dismantled the bomb that was found on the boat.'

A gasp of excitement rippled round the hall, and several boys scrabbled to unbuckle their satchels, pulling out pens and paper. Rory even heard one of the girls say, 'This is going to be the best lesson we've had all year.'

Chapter 21

Straight after assembly, Rory and Paul, as honorary invalids, were helped into the front seat of the RAF truck. Tom and Charlie were boosted up to travel in the back. At the base, tall double gates, bound with prickly barbed wire, swung open to let them in. They were to join a small group of men, who were also going to be shown around. Rory recognised the man directing the tour as the Padre – a friend of his father.

'We cannot, of course, for reasons of security, show areas of current action,' he was saying, 'but I thought you might like to visit our repair shop in Hangar Two. We're working on one of our Lancaster bombers, so you'll be able to see it close up. It was damaged on its last sortie. However, it will give you some idea of the difference in size – from the seemingly small aircraft you see flying over your heads, to what they are like on the ground.'

Rory glanced at Paul, whose eyes were shining. This was going to beat any picture in a war magazine.

Tagging onto the end of the group, they crossed the tarmac, turning to feast envious eyes on the distant line up of active planes, out of bounds to the public at the other end of the airfield.

The hangar they entered was huge. It echoed like a dark cave, and exuded a heady smell of engine oil. Best of all, towering over them in the gloom, with wings outstretched high above, like a great monstrous bat, was an actual Lancaster bomber.

At ground level the twin wheels of the undercarriage were as wide as overturned beer barrels. Looking up at the bomb bay from underneath, Rory thought the whole plane must be as high as a house. Mechanics in blue overalls crawled all over it, busy working on the engines, and repairing the fuselage. One of the wings had a neat line of holes punched across it. Where else, Rory wondered, might other bullets have gone? Then, with a jolt of surprise, he nudged Paul and turned to the Padre.

'Was this the one we saw come in the other morning, with its engine on fire?'

'Yes, this would be it. We were happy it managed to limp home with the crew intact,' said the Padre. 'If you like, we can go up the gangway and take a look inside. You'll be surprised how cramped it is in there, so I'm afraid looking in is all we'll be able to do.'

The gangway was narrow, and the boys were last in the queue. Rory used his waiting time to look around. A spray of sparks caught his eye. A mechanic on a ladder was welding something. He looked a bit like a voodoo witchdoctor, behind the black metal mask he held to protect his face. Another spray of sparks. As they died down, job completed, the man lowered his shield.

Blue overalls were no disguise. Rory recognised the fair hair, that distinctive face. His heartbeat quickened. He nudged Paul and pointed. Paul gripped Rory's arm, and they watched as the man rested his welding torch on the engine cowling. Wiping perspiration from his brow, Sven suddenly caught them staring. He moved fast. Leaping to the ground, he ran for the hangar door.

'Get him!' shouted Rory, alerting Charlie and Tom. They took off and veered to the right, behind a parked truck. As Sven came by, Charlie's practiced boot shot out to trip him up. Sven slammed to the ground, banging his head on the concrete floor.

'Hold him!' shouted Rory, running over.

Boiling with rage, Rory leapt onto Sven's back. Swinging his great awkward plaster, he hit him hard on the back of his head, crying, 'That's for my mum!'

All that talk about only wanting to use the new bomb as a threat to make the war stop had been rubbish. Here he was, once more in another place he'd no right to be, planning more sabotage, but on a plane this time. It was all Rory could do to stop himself from hitting him again.

The line of grown-ups were looking down at them, with their mouths open in amazement.

'This man is a spy!' shouted Rory in explanation. 'Someone fetch the police!'

Sven lay quite still. Was he dead? Rory's anger was drowned out by a feeling of horror. His breath came in frightened gasps. What had he done? With a shaking hand, he felt along Sven's limp wrist for a pulse, but without knowing how to do it properly, he could sense nothing.

Around him, mechanics were scrambling down from the plane. Someone was on a walkie–talkie. There was the noise of a jeep skidding on gravel as it pulled up outside. Three white-capped, RAF police jumped out and bundled into the hangar.

'What's going on here?' barked one of them.

'We recognised this man as the spy, he's the one who put a bomb on a boat in our harbour. His name's Sven and I think he was trying to sabotage your plane. I hit him and…' Rory gulped, hesitated, then whispered, '…and I think that maybe he's dead.'

The man bent down and felt for a pulse.

'No such luck, lad. He'll survive. You've just knocked him out.'

The group of adults had now come back down the gangway, and stood staring at them. The Padre, having had to extricate himself from the narrow innards of the plane, pushed past them to come over.

'Boys!' he said, looking bewildered, 'I'd only been gone a minute.'

Another jeep arrived outside the hanger, pulling up with a squeal of brakes. The Wing Commander stepped out.

'Good Lord! I did wonder whether Sir John's idea of allowing schoolboys on a tour was a good idea, but they tell me this is your spy, so I might even ask you to visit again.'

It took Rory a minute to realise that the Wing Commander wasn't cross. He was making a joke.

An ambulance arrived, and Sven's limp body was stretchered into it. The doctor who'd come with the ambulance looked over. Seeing Rory clutching his plastered arm, he came to examine it.

'You're not meant to hit people with your plaster, young man. That arm will need an X-ray to see if it should be reset. Hop aboard.' The doctor jerked a thumb at Sven's limp body, and Rory's heart skipped a beat. 'This chap needs to be checked out in hospital too, before he ends up in The Clink.'

Rory had read about how spies were shot by a firing squad, but he suddenly realised that he didn't want Sven to die. It would be too easy for him. At least if he was locked up he'd have time to think about what he'd done. Maybe he'd even repent. From the window, he could see Paul, Charlie and Tom regaling the other members of the guided

tour with the tale of their previous adventure. At least they were still having fun. As he caught a last glance of the giant Lancaster bomber, looming in the darkness of the hangar, he felt glad. He hadn't been able to help it last time, but at least he'd saved it from Sven.

*****

At the hospital, the RAF doctor showed Rory into the outpatients' department and explained about the X-ray to the receptionist. Someone was going to contact his dad. That would take ages. Rory's arm wasn't hurting so badly now, just a bit of an ache, but after waiting for half an hour, he was thoroughly bored.

To the right was a ward full of busy nurses, but on his left was an empty chair, standing in the doorway of a single room. Inside, still unconscious, lay Sven. Rory froze, for around Sven's wrist was a metal bracelet. He'd been handcuffed to the bed. Rory hesitated a minute longer, then he crept over to the bedside. He stood, looking down at his friend.

'I'm sorry,' he whispered.

Sven's eyelids fluttered open. A small smile flickered round his lips, and the fingers of his free hand rippled in a weak wave.

'Not your fault.' The words were a whisper. 'Maybe one day we still go climb these cliffs.' Sven's eyes closed again, on a faint smile, but he lay still once more. The effort to speak had been too much.

'Oi! What you doing in here?'

Rory spun round. An RAF policeman barged into the room, trying to grab him. Ducking under his arm, Rory took off and rocketed down the corridor.

As he ran, Rory thought about Sven. Yes, he had hit him. Yes, he'd seen him in the ambulance. But all he'd wanted was for him to be caught. Sven had been his friend. And when he'd spoken, just then, he didn't seem to hold it against him. What would happen to him now?

'Rory!'

Dad was at the waiting room door, and there behind him was Mum. Of course! She was safe now that Sven had been caught. She could even come back home. Thank goodness, they could go all back to normal.

Hugging someone with an arm in a heavy plaster cast was pretty impossible, but at least Mum could get her arms around him. It was stupid, but he just wanted to stay there. To his horror, he felt, hot tears well up.

Mum must have felt him tremble, because she murmured to him softly, 'Don't worry, Love. You're just suffering from shock.'

Feeling better, he looked up at her, 'Mum, what will happen to Sven?'

'He'll go to prison, but I think they may give him the option of returning to Norway to spy for our side.'

'You mean, like a double agent?'

'Most spies are either in it for the money or for the adventure. Very few are really dedicated to the cause they represent. I think your Sven is first and last a Norwegian. Deep down, he probably really resents the Nazis occupying his country.'

'But...'

'Rory Mackay?' a nurse was calling him for his X-ray.

The black and white picture of his arm bones was fascinating, but according to the doctor, despite everything, the cast had been strong enough to hold them in place. He could go home. Dad led him out to an RAF jeep.

'Now, Rory,' said Dad. 'Sit in that front seat for a minute, while I get something.' He scrabbled about in his pocket, and brought out one of his thick black pencils. Leaning forward, he began to write something on Rory's plaster.

'It's upside down for me,' protested Rory. 'what have you written?'

'I've written *that's my boy!* and I've signed it: *By his dad: Kenneth Mackay.*'

Rory grinned, and his mum laughed. Dad had really changed.

'Oh, and as you missed school today, Mr Campbell sent you some homework.'

Rory couldn't believe his ears. So nothing much had changed at all, then.

'It's maths,' said Dad. 'I used to be good at that, so maybe I could give you a hand. We could do it together.'

'Yeah, Dad,' said Rory with a wide grin, 'I think I'd like that.'

GLOSSARY

Ack-ack guns: A gun designed to shoot upwards at aeroplanes.

Amphibian: Army vehicle shaped like a boat, that could also run on land.

Berth: A place reserved for a boat in a harbour.

Brae: Scottish word for a steep bank.

Blackout: In wartime no light could be shown at night, for fear of attracting enemy aeroplanes.

Black Market: Illegal selling of rationed items.

Commandos: Soldiers specially trained to carry out raids.

Coast Guard Station: Office for lookouts, keeping watch for danger at sea.

Char lady: Old fashioned name for a cleaner.

Caterpillar tracks: A belt of metal plates around the wheels of army tanks, to prevent them sinking into mud.

Children's Hour: An hour long radio programme for children, broadcast every week day between 5-6 pm.

Clink: An old name for a prison.

Double Agent: A spy who, working for one government, is really spying for another.

Evacuees: Children sent to live in the countryside, to be safe from the bombs falling on cities.

Forces' Canteen: A cafe for soldiers, sailors, and airmen, set up in villages where they've been stationed.

Flounder: A type of flat fish.

Gum: Chewing gum was something that American serviceman brought to Britain where sweets were rationed.

Go-kart: A soap-box go-kart is an open wheeled buggie, propelled only by gravity down a slope.

Grace: A prayer of thanks said before a meal.

Jerry: A slang word for the German war time enemy.

Ja: The Norwegian word for 'yes.'

Jack knifed: To fall like a high diver.

Live Rounds: Bullets and explosives ready to go off.

Lewis Gun: A light weight double barrelled machine gun.

La-di-dah: Upper class accent.

Lerwick: The main town on the Shetland Islands.

Mooring ropes: The ropes used to tie a boat to the quay.

Manse: The house where the church minister lives in

Scotland. A vicarage is the English equivalent.

Marram grass: A tough grass, planted on sand dunes to stop the wind blowing the sand away.

Morse Code: A system for sending messages using long and short sounds to represent letters and numbers.

Nazis: German followers of Adolf Hitler who started the Second World War.

Pier: A landing place for ships, sometimes built on posts out over the water.

Potato Holidays: An October school holiday given in war time, for children to help with the potato harvest.

Polio: An infectious disease that can leave limbs paralysed.

Paraffin stove: A simple cooking stove powered by paraffin oil, used in most kitchens before electricity and gas became available.

Quay: The dock running alongside the water to load and unload people and cargo from ships.

Queen Boudica: Was the Queen of the British Iceni tribe who fought against the invading Romans.

Refugees: People seeking safety from danger, usually caused by war.

Red Cross: A medical charity, usually active in war time.

Ration Book: A book of coupons allowing the owner to have a measured amount of essentials like food. In wartime food ships were bombed by the enemy, so what did get through was shared out, or rationed, to make sure everyone got the same amount.

RAF Base: A Royal Air Force airfield.

Spitfire: British fighter aircraft.

Squadron: A unit of airmen and their planes.

Spastic: Unkind slang word for a disabled person.

Trawler: A fishing boat that catches fish, by pulling a net behind it.

W.R.V.S: Women's Royal Volunteer Service - groups of women who give their time free to help people. They were very active during the war.

Wash House: A place with a boiler where one could wash clothes before washing machines were invented.

Wireless: the first name for a radio, as it didn't need a wire connection like a telephone.

Historical Note

In 1939, Germany invaded Poland. In retaliation, Britain declared war on Germany.

Over the next year, 1940, Germany went on to take over Denmark and Norway. Many Norwegians fled in fishing boats, crossing the North Sea to find safety in Scotland. Some of those left behind formed themselves into a secret underground movement, designed to fight the Germans.

In Scotland, a unit was set up on the Shetland Islands to help support this resistance. Fishing boats, braving terrible storms, took over supplies of arms and explosives. On their return, they brought back refugees escaping from the Germans. This secret wartime mission came to be called The Shetland Bus. Some of their fishing boats operated out of other Scottish harbours. "The Kirsten", in our story, would have been one of those.

During the early years of the war it was feared that Germany might invade Britain by coming over from Norway, landing in the North East of Scotland. Beaches were cordoned off and mined. Some of these sandy beaches were similar to those in Normandy, so later Army exercises held there served two purposes. Firstly, they were practice for the real D-day landings in French Normandy. Secondly, they were designed to misdirect the Germans, making them think that the Allies would attempt to retake Europe via Norway.

In the story, Dougie refers to an actual incident when three German spies – a woman and two men – dropped along the Moray Firth coast, not far from Rory's village, and were arrested. In the next year, 1941, two more German spies were dropped along the same coast. Those two, however, went straight to the police station, offering instead to spy for Britain against the Germans. They were the ones who sent the misinformation that the Allies planned to attack Europe by landing in Norway. This probably persuaded Hitler to keep 250,000 troops there, rather than sending them to Normandy where the real attack was to occur.

Ration books

During World War Two, everybody had to have a ration book if they wanted to buy food. There were blue ones for children and cream coloured ones for adults. Food was very scarce. Each purchase had to be bought with money and a coupon which was cut from the book.

Hitler knew that Britain imported a great deal of its food. Wheat came from Canada and America. Bananas and dried fruit came from across the seas, as did all the other things like rice that don't grow in the UK. Ships trying to bring food in by ship were attacked by Hitler's submarines. He could have won the war by starving the people of Britain.

Lord Woolton, the Minister for Food, was a clever man. He worked out how much food a healthy person should have each day. Everyone was to have the same amount of meat, butter, tea, bacon, and sugar. Children could have sweets, but only so many each week. The idea was that what was available should be shared equally between everyone, despite how much money they had. It was an excellent idea and it worked very well.

The Black Market

As usual there were some people only too keen to have more than their share. This encouraged criminals to steal batches of food and offer it around at a high price.

Hopefully all of the above gives you a good idea of what wartime life was like.